Heads up!

"Hey, Joe! Everyone! Get off the field." Frank quickly pulled a few people out of the way and pushed them toward an exit. As the whining canister neared them, more people noticed it. Joe joined Frank in herding people to safety. Finally they headed for the exit themselves.

"Hit the deck!" Joe yelled as he looked back one last time. The metal missile was about to crash into the ground. "Now!" Once inside the large exit ramp, Frank and Joe dove for the floor.

With a deafening thud, the canister hit the ground and shattered. Pieces of metal shrapnel flew around the field. A couple of shouts from the vicinity of the band told Frank that some lethal pieces might have hit that area.

"Are you okay?" Joe asked, scrambling to his feet.

The Hardy Boys Mystery Stories

#141 The Desert Thieves

#143 The Giant Rat of Sumatra

#152 Danger in the Extreme

#153 Eye on Crime

#154 The Caribbean Cruise Caper

#156 A Will to Survive

#159 Daredevils

#160 A Game Called Chaos

#161 Training for Trouble

#162 The End of the Trail

#163 The Spy That Never Lies

#164 Skin & Bones

#165 Crime in the Cards

#166 Past and Present Danger

#167 Trouble Times Two

#168 The Castle Conundrum

#169 Ghost of a Chance

#170 Kickoff to Danger

#171 The Test Case

#172 Trouble in Warp Space

#173 Speed Times Five

#174 Hide-and-Sneak

#175 Trick-or-Trouble

#176 In Plane Sight

#177 The Case of the Psychic's Vision

#178 The Mystery of the Black Rhino

#179 Passport to Danger

The Hardy Boys Ghost Stories

Available from ALADDIN Paperbacks

THE **HARDY BOYS**®

#179
PASSPORT TO DANGER

FRANKLIN W. DIXON

Aladdin Paperbacks
New York London Toronto Sydney Singapore

This book is a work of fiction. Any references to historical events, real people, or real locales are used fictitiously. Other names, characters, places, and incidents are the product of the author's imagination, and any resemblance to actual events or locales or persons, living or dead, is entirely coincidental.

First Aladdin Paperbacks edition June 2003
Copyright © 2003 by Simon & Schuster, Inc.

ALADDIN PAPERBACKS
An imprint of Simon & Schuster
Children's Publishing Division
1230 Avenue of the Americas
New York, NY 10020

The text of this book was set in New Caledonia.

Printed in the United States of America
2 4 6 8 10 9 7 5 3 1

THE HARDY BOYS MYSTERY STORIES is a trademark of Simon & Schuster, Inc.

THE HARDY BOYS and colophon are registered trademarks of Simon & Schuster, Inc.

Library of Congress Control Number 2002115454

ISBN 0-689-85779-9

Contents

1	*A Deadly Dud*	1
2	*Red Card Up*	11
3	*Foul Play*	19
4	*A Clue of Gold*	28
5	*Hanging with Marie*	37
6	*Gimme an M?*	44
7	*Gimme a W?*	51
8	*Yellow Card Up*	61
9	*The Art of Detecting*	72
10	*Without a Trace*	79
11	*GPS Says Yes*	89
12	*Breakaway to Danger*	96
13	*And Then There Were Two*	107
14	*Buried with the Bones*	118
15	*The Quarry in the Quarry*	129
16	*Kickoff!*	140

PASSPORT TO DANGER

1 A Deadly Dud

"Joe—watch out!" Frank Hardy yelled at his brother. "Duck!"

The warning came too late. With a juicy splat, a huge red tomato smashed into Joe Hardy's face. When it hit, he knew instantly why it was so big: The tomato was swollen with rot. The smell of it filled his nostrils as he wiped bits of greenish black pulp from his clear blue eyes.

"Man, this is gross," Joe complained, spitting out a few foul-tasting slimy seeds.

Frank fought back the grin as long as possible. He couldn't help smiling, even though he knew if it had happened to him, he wouldn't think it was funny.

Sometimes people didn't realize at first that the Hardys were brothers, because they looked so different. Eighteeen-year-old Frank was taller, with short, straight dark hair and brown eyes. A year younger, Joe had wavy blond hair, and although he was shorter, he had a stronger build.

"Hey, I'm really sorry about that." A man who looked like he was in his late twenties handed Joe a towel. "This place is a zoo today, as you Americans say." He was tall with light brown hair and bright blue-green eyes, and he spoke English with a French accent. "I'm Jacques Ravel, here to work the tournament. Are you volunteers too?"

Joe wiped the tomato juice off his face and nodded. They were standing in front of Le Stade de France, the world-class soccer stadium in Paris. Since their team's masterful capture of the World Cup in 1998, the French were crazier about the sport than ever—if that were possible. A noisy crowd clustered around the stadium entrance.

"I'm Frank Hardy, and this is my brother, Joe. We're on the equipment team for the Americans." The Hardys had been invited to work as volunteers at a four-team world amateur invitational soccer tournament held in Paris. It was a sunny Wednesday morning, and they were reporting for their orientation meeting.

"So what are they so excited—or bothered—about?" Frank asked, nodding toward the noisy crowd.

"Which group?" Jacques replied with his own

question. "We seem to have two sets of protestors today." He shrugged as though he wasn't surprised by the crowds.

"Let's start with the ones who are pitching the rotten vegetables," Joe said, shaking out the towel.

Jacques pointed out where the clusters of protestors seemed to be divided. "Those would be Isabelle's gang," he said, pointing to the left of the stadium's entrance. "See, there she is—the one with the long red hair. That's Isabelle Genet."

Frank spotted the woman Jacques pointed out. She looked like she was maybe forty years old, and she had a hard, mean look. She was dressed in camouflage clothing and combat boots. She was yelling in French, but Frank could understand most of it.

"She's talking about Victoire, right?" Frank translated. "Is that the name of her group? Victory?"

"Very good," Jacques said, nodding. "Victoire started out as a nice friendly group interested in preserving the history of our beautiful city. They wanted Paris to keep her flavor as an old-world capital, but still function as a force in the twenty-first century."

"Oh, yeah," Joe said, wiping the last bit of tomato off his green T-shirt. "They're real nice and friendly."

"Well, she actually sounds pretty friendly," Frank said, listening intently to Isabelle. "She's talking about not wanting Paris to be like London, with smog and sewage in the river." He was quiet for a minute

3

or two, then his eyes widened. "Whoa," he said, then continued listening. "I see what you mean, Jacques."

"What's she saying?" Joe asked. "My French is way rusty."

"Well, she seems to be calling for Victoire to destroy Le Stade. Have I got that right?" he asked Jacques. "She wants to destroy the stadium?"

"That's pretty much what she's saying," Jacques said with another shrug. "They see the construction of our space-age stadium as a huge setback to their cause. So their answer is to tear it down. But it's never going to happen," he concluded.

"What about that group?" Joe asked, pointing to the smaller crowd on the right side of the entrance.

"Absolutely no competition for Isabelle," Jacques said. As he spoke, a very tall, thin man stepped forward holding a small microphone. He looked distinguished, dressed in a suit and tie, with perfectly combed hair. "That's Auguste Bergerac," Jacques continued. "He was a pretty big deal, as you Americans say. He was once a local politician, but he was recently voted out of his office. He is quickly becoming a has-been." Jacques pronounced the last word with a long *E* sound, like the word "bean."

"He seems to be blaming a lot of different people and groups for what happened to him," Frank said. "Mostly the opposing party, I take it."

"Yes," Jacques said. "He blames everyone but himself."

"So why is he here?" Joe asked. "What's *his* beef against Le Stade?"

"Nothing against the stadium specifically, probably," Jacques explained. "But he wants to keep his name alive."

"So what better place than the venue for the international amateur soccer tournament," Frank added.

"Exactly," Jacques agreed.

"You know a lot about what's going on around here," Frank said. "I take it you're a Parisian."

"I am," Jacques said. "Lived here all my life."

"Speaking of the tournament, let's get inside," Joe said. "I'm ready to get to work." He started for the door, keeping his eyes on the vegetable-wielding protestors.

"Space-age is right," Frank murmured, as they entered Le Stade.

The Hardys had driven by the stadium, but no view from outside could begin to do it justice. The enormous elliptical bowl was topped by a roof that looked sort of like frosted glass. It was open to the sky in the center and also open all around the top of the stadium.

The roof seemed to be floating above the field. A closer look showed that it was balanced on top of eighteen steel pillars shooting up about a hundred and fifty feet into the air. It looked as if someone just dropped the roof down and perched it on those pillars.

It was just as noisy on the field as it was outside the stadium, but the commotion was much friendlier. A couple of teams were scrimmaging.

Other groups in the stadium were preparing for the next day's opening ceremonies. Behind the goalposts at one end, dancers rehearsed to rock music being played by a band up in the stands. Behind the opposite goal posts, a fireworks crew worked through their routine, occasionally sending up a trial rocket. Sound and lighting technicians tested their equipment around the stadium.

The Hardys and the other volunteers reported to a mess tent set up at the side of the field. The volunteer coordinator met with them first. "*Bonjour,* everyone. I am Henri. Look around this incredible building. It is a marvel of modern construction. The roof alone weighs thirteen tons—that's as much as the Eiffel Tower!"

His arm swept through the air, gesturing toward the lower rows of the stand. "The stands are divided into three layers," he said. "Right now—for the soccer game—they are all in view. But if we wanted a larger arena, the whole bank of lower stands is retractable. All twenty-five thousand of those seats can be rolled back on a cushion of air, steel, and rollers. And they disappear under the middle stands."

The volunteers spent the rest of the morning touring the facility. They checked out the locker rooms and equipment facilities and learned all the safety and evacuation procedures.

When lunch break was called, the Hardys joined the others at the mess tent. Frank and Joe took their places in the line that snaked around the food table. They filled their plates with sandwiches and heaps of *pommes frites*—the original French fries. Then they picked up some juice and wandered over toward the tables.

"Frank, Joe—over here," Jacques called from a table in the corner. The Hardys took the two remaining empty chairs, and Jacques introduced the others at the table. A few were also volunteers, but most were American and British players and coaches.

"So, are we all pumped about this tournament or what?" Joe said with a big grin. He had loved sports all his life, and soccer was one of his favorites. As if to answer his question, a sudden burst of crackling fireworks sounded from the other end of the field.

"Absolutely," answered one of the British assistant coaches. "This is like a launching pad for us. Today, we are amateurs, tomorrow we are pros!"

"So where are you all staying?" Jacques asked. "I know they set up dorms for some of the players at schools."

Everyone answered at once. The volunteers who didn't live in Paris seemed to be spread out all over the city, staying with family, friends, or strangers who had opened their homes to the visitors.

"We're sleeping in the players' dorm," said one of the American players.

"We're staying with a friend of the family," Joe told the others. He and Frank exchanged looks. Joe didn't mention that their father, Fenton Hardy, was in Paris too, attending a top-secret symposium on security for sports events.

A former ace detective with the New York City Police Department, Fenton had opened a private detective agency in Bayport. He was now considered one of the best private investigators in America. Frank and Joe had inherited his skill at cracking cases, and they often assisted him.

"There's no way we could be in a dorm," a young British player answered. "Coach Roberts always insists we stay somewhere apart—"

As if on cue, a burly man in a bright red jacket stormed up to the table. He had dark blue eyes, and hair the steely color of a medieval sword. Frank recognized him immediately as Montgomery Roberts, coach of the British team.

"Garber. Horton. Brantley. Waltham." Coach Roberts barked out the names as if he were a drill sergeant at roll call. "Meeting in five minutes."

Joe stood up and extended his hand. "Coach Roberts," he said, "it's an honor to meet one of the greatest soccer coaches of all time! I'm Joe Hardy, and this is my brother, Frank."

The coach's beefy hand gripped Joe's firmly, and pumped it once. Then he nodded at Frank, turned, and stomped away. The players and coaches whose names he'd called out stood up quickly and took their plates to the mess counter. Then they followed Roberts to the locker room.

"So that's Montgomery Roberts," Frank said.

"Also known as 'Magnificent Montie, Soccer Legend,'" Joe added. "He's one of the most successful coaches in soccer. He's a strict coach—a real taskmaster. But he's a genius, and he knows how to get the job done."

"Also known as 'Monster Montie,' a legend of another sort," Jacques countered. "Some say he's a bully and a tyrant and will do just about anything to ensure that his team has the upper hand. I think I'll follow along. Maybe I can get an exclusive."

"You're a reporter?" Frank asked.

"Yes," Jacques said in a low voice. "But keep it our secret. I'm doing some undercover work, posing as a volunteer. I want to get the real inside story of the tournament—not just the same stories that everyone else gets."

A low voice boomed a sentence in French through the stadium speaker system. That was followed by the same sentence in Spanish, then in English: "Volunteers, please report to your captains for afternoon orientation."

"Cover for me?" Jacques asked. "If anyone asks,

tell them I'll be right back." Frank and Joe deposited their lunch trays and dishes on the mess counter and left the tent. The music revved up, filling the air with high-pitched guitar whines and pounding bass thumps. Frank could feel the vibrations in his stomach and instinctively nodded his head to the beat. Then another noise pierced through the music. It was a higher pitch than the lead guitar, more of a tight squeal. And it seemed to be coming from near the locker room.

Shielding his eyes from the sun, Frank looked up toward the band, but the sound wasn't coming from there. It was behind him, and it was getting louder. The sound began to chase all the other noises out of the stadium; it filled his ears. Frank wheeled around. Streaming down from the sky with a whistling whine was a large metal canister about the size of a bucket—and it was coming right at him.

2 Red Card Up

"Hey, Joe! Everyone! Get off the field." Frank quickly pulled a few people out of the way and pushed them toward an exit. As the whining canister neared them, more people noticed it. Joe joined Frank in herding people to safety. Finally they headed for the exit themselves.

"Hit the deck!" Joe yelled as he looked back one last time. The metal missile was about to crash into the ground. "Now!" Once inside the large exit ramp, Frank and Joe dove for the floor.

With a deafening thud, the canister hit the ground and shattered. Pieces of metal shrapnel flew around the field. A couple of shouts from the vicinity of the band told Frank that some lethal pieces might have hit that area.

"Are you okay?" Joe asked, scrambling to his feet.

"Yeah," Frank said. "Anybody hurt out there?" he called out.

There were a few grumbles from around the stadium, but no screams of pain.

The Hardys walked back onto the field and checked out what was left of the strange missile. Joe touched a piece of it with the toe of his shoe. "What do you think—"

"Fireworks," Frank interrupted. He looked down toward the opposite goalpost. Two members of the fireworks crew were running across the field toward them. "Look," he said, pointing to them. "I'll bet it was an unexploded firework."

"I'll go check out the band," Joe said. "I think I heard some yells when the thing exploded." He streaked up the aisle steps to where the band had been rehearsing.

When the two men from the fireworks crew reached Frank, they were frantic and chattered nonstop to each other and to him—at first in quick Italian. "English?" Frank asked. "Do either of you speak English?"

"I," one of the men said. "I speak English." He wore faded blue coveralls with a patch on the front pocket that read MACRI MAGNIFICO on the first line and SYLVIO on the second.

"Your name is Sylvio?" Frank asked. When the man nodded, Frank continued his questions. "What happened? Was this part of a firework?" He pointed to the small hole in the ground and the pieces of twisted metal.

"Yes, yes, yes," Sylvio said. "An accident, a terrible accident. We don't know how it happened. We have called the medics. They will be here soon."

"I'll take it from here," another man said, coming up behind Frank. He spoke English, but with a heavy French accent. "I am Officer Binet." Frank saw the stadium security badge on the man's jacket. "Are you hurt?" he asked Frank. "Is anyone hurt?"

"Joe?" Frank called out to his brother. "How's it look up there?"

"We've got some injured here," Joe said. Frank watched as his brother helped some of the players lie down, took pulses, and covered the bass player with a jacket.

Frank listened as Officer Binet interviewed the fireworks crew members, but they didn't offer any more than he'd already heard. Then he and the officer joined Joe in the stands. A few of the players had minor shrapnel wounds from the metal that had exploded. When the EMTs arrived, they patched up the wounded before taking them to the hospital. Frank and Joe finished giving their statements to Officer Binet, and then he left.

"Looks like they're getting back to work," Joe noted as they walked across the field. The volunteer squad was slowly gathering under the goalposts.

"Come on," Frank said. "I want to check the fireworks setup first."

"What are you thinking?" Joe asked.

"I don't know," Frank said. "We've got demonstrators outside threatening to mess up the tournament and saying they're going to tear down the stadium. Then suddenly there's this so-called accident. I just want to check it out."

The Hardys walked around the edge of the field to the opposite end where the fireworks crew had set up. A large trailer stood about forty yards from the field and anchored the small compound. On the side of the trailer were pictures of exploding fireworks and the words MACRI MAGNIFICO. Nearby was a small tent full of electronic equipment.

"Hi, Sylvio," Frank said, spotting the man he'd talked to earlier. "Did you figure out what happened?"

"No, no, no," the man said. He was sitting at a small console with a computer and an electronic display monitor. "We don't know," Sylvio added. "We're trying to find out."

Joe walked over to the console. It looked like the kind of sound equipment he'd seen at concerts. Frank wandered over to join him.

"So you run this whole show with computers?" Joe said, surveying the setup. "Is that how you coordinate the launches?"

"*Si.* Yes," Sylvio answered, nodding. He seemed

very nervous. "It's all computers now. They say which fireworks we fire, when we fire them, how high they go, when they explode—everything. It's all very . . . very . . . it's precision, you know? So no accidents, no mistakes."

"Unless someone messes with the computer," Joe said under his breath.

"You better go," Sylvio said. "Mr. Macri told us that no one should talk about this. I don't want to be fired. I need my job."

"No problem," Frank said. "It's okay. We won't tell anyone you talked to us." He couldn't shake the notion that Sylvio knew more than he was saying. Frank scribbled the phone number of the apartment where the Hardys were staying on a corner of paper he tore from his volunteer notebook. "If you get in trouble, just let us know. We'll stand up for you. And feel free to call us if you find out anything more. We'll never tell who told us."

Sylvio shook his head, but he pocketed the scrap of paper.

As the Hardys left the Macri fireworks compound, Joe saw something in a short hedge, glinting in the sun. He reached under the green leaves and pulled out what looked like a small gold soccer ball. It was bigger than a charm—more like something hanging off a key chain. "Anybody drop this?" he called back to the crew, holding it up. No one stepped forward, so Joe dropped it in his pocket.

The Hardys rejoined the volunteer squads and went back to work. "Okay, so we had a minor accident this morning with the unexploded firework canister," the volunteer coordinator was saying as they walked up. "We're lucky there wasn't a big crowd here. But even if there had been, this stadium has a lot of features that can handle security problems."

He told them to open their security and evacuation guides. "Remember what you learned this morning. Although Le Stade can hold up to a hundred thousand spectators, they can all be evacuated in fifteen minutes because of the unique layout of the exits. If this incident had occurred when we had a full house, we would be counting on you to help with the safe and orderly removal of specatators. Okay, everybody, break into your individual teams and familiarize yourselves with your jobs."

Joe and Frank followed their team captain to the sidelines. When the captain called for someone to go to one of the locker rooms to gather more towels, Frank eagerly volunteered. "I'm going to take a detour through the fireworks setup," he told Joe in a low voice. "Cover for me if the captain starts to wonder where I am."

When Frank reached the area that Macri Magnifico had staked out for their operations, most of the crew was gone. Frank was relieved to see that only Sylvio was still hanging around.

"Oh no, oh no," Sylvio said when he saw Frank

walking toward him. "We're not supposed to talk to anyone. Strict orders from Mr. Macri. No talking."

"Just tell me if they've found anything suspicious," Frank said. "I won't let anyone know how I found out."

"Ah, what difference does it make anyway?" Sylvio cried, throwing his hands up. "I'm probably going to be fired. It's my program, so it's my fault."

"Program?" Frank said, his attention focused. "Do you mean the computer program?"

"*Si*," Sylvio said. "*Si*, the program. They think it was my mistake, but it wasn't. The program is different from what I created. It's been changed. Someone has written in new trajectories—new flight plans for the effects."

"That throws off your whole plan, right?" Frank asked.

"*Si*. That's what happened on the field. The canister didn't go high enough. It came down too soon, before it exploded in the air. It was like a bomb when it landed—like a grenade." Sylvio closed his eyes and then looked back at Frank. "We don't know how much damage is done to my program. We may have to cancel everything for tomorrow night. It's terrible. Terrible!"

"Who could have access to your program?" Frank asked.

"No one!" Sylvio said. "It's secure!" He was getting more agitated. "Go now," he told Frank. "I am

17

already in trouble. I will be in more trouble if they see me talking to you."

Frank backed out of the tent. "No problem," he said. "Remember, I'm on your side. You have my number. Call me if you find out anything." He couldn't tell whether Sylvio trusted him enough to call or not. But he knew it was worth a try to encourage him to call.

Frank hurried to the locker room to get the towels, which were kept in a corner linen closet. The room was quiet when Frank opened the door. Dim and shadowy, it was lit by only one small overhead security light that indicated the location of the exit.

As Frank reached for the light switch, he noticed a bulky silhouette ahead. It looked like a figure kneeling near one of the benches in front of a bank of lockers. Without taking his eyes off the figure, Frank quietly closed the door behind him, but the click of the latch startled the kneeling figure. The person jumped up, and Frank slammed his hand into the light switch.

As light bathed the room, a figure in bright red disappeared around the lockers toward another exit. Frank hurried to the bench where the person had been kneeling. His heart was pounding; he was sure he wasn't going to like what he saw.

He was right. There, sprawled on the floor next to the bench, was the Brazilian amateur soccer coach, Gabriel Sant'Anna.

3 Foul Play

"Coach! Can you hear me?" Frank called to the still body on the floor. He checked the man's pulse. "Whew." Frank let out a breath of relief. "His pulse isn't very strong," he said to himself, "but at least he's got one."

As Frank was checking the coach, the door behind him opened. "Hey," Frank said, getting to his feet. "I need some help. Coach Sant—"

The slamming door interrupted Frank's words. He rushed to see who'd been there, but the hall outside was empty. Whoever had rushed out the door was gone.

Frank ran to the security phone on the wall and called for help. Then he went back to the unconscious coach. He knew better than to move the man or try to revive him with water. But he also knew that sometimes even unconscious people can hear. So he continued to talk to Coach Sant'Anna and assure him that help was on the way.

As Frank talked, he looked around. The coach's left hand was twisted awkwardly under his leg. Lying under a nearby bench was a blue pen.

The paramedics and a stadium security officer arrived quickly. Frank told the security officer what had happened and about the figure he'd seen running out of the locker room. The officer called the Paris police, then took off along the the path the mysterious person had taken.

The paramedics administered an IV of fluids and medicines to Coach Sant'Anna and loaded him onto a gurney. When they lifted the coach's body, Frank spotted a faint blue line on the floor. As the medics wheeled the gurney to the ambulance waiting outside, Frank knelt back down next to the bench.

Three more blue lines were scratched on the floor under where the coach's hand had been twisted. Together the lines formed a capital *M*.

"Frank!" Joe's voice echoed around the banks of lockers. "Frank! You in here?"

"Over here," Frank called out. He stood to greet his brother, Jacques, and a few other volunteers.

"Are you all right?" Jacques asked. "We saw the medics come in, then roll someone out."

"It was Coach Sant'Anna," Frank said. He decided to keep all the details to himself for the moment. "I found him unconscious," he said. "I don't know what happened."

"This day has been one of calamity," Jacques observed, running his hand through his hair. "You Americans say it well: It has been *unreal*. Come on. We have to tell the rest of the crew what happened."

"You all go ahead," Joe said. "I'll help Frank get the towels."

Jacques and the others returned to the field. Frank gathered the towels he'd come to get and filled in Joe on the details of what had happened.

"Do you think this means anything?" Joe asked, looking at the faint blue *M* on the floor.

"Maybe," Frank answered. "His hand was twisted under his body pretty near that spot, and the blue pen is under the bench."

"Yeah, but coaches use those markers all the time to set up plays on their clipboards. That pen could have been dropped by anyone at any time. And that looks like an *M*, but it could be just four scratchy lines. Maybe somebody stepped on the open pen and skidded it back and forth across the floor."

"Maybe," Frank said with a nod.

When the stadium security officer returned, Frank showed him the pen and the marks on the floor. The officer carefully picked up the pen, looked at the blue marks, and shrugged. Then he escorted Frank and Joe out of the room and closed the door.

"Okay," Joe said, as they walked along the hall toward the tunnel leading to the field. "So you see somebody with kind of a stocky figure, wearing a red jacket, and in the same room as Coach Sant'Anna's unconscious body. Then you find an *M* scratched on the floor. So we're thinking Sant'Anna might have been scratching out *M* for 'Montie,' right? Big, red-jacket-wearing Coach Montie Roberts?"

"It adds up so far, but we still don't have enough information," Frank said. "At this point, it's just a good guess."

"We need more facts," Joe agreed.

"And I'd like to know who popped in the door and ran back out so fast without a word," Frank added. "That was definitely weird."

Back on the field, they had little time for more speculation. So much time had been lost by the incidents with the fireworks and Coach Sant'Anna, the volunteers had to work fast to finish their orientation and instructions. While they were completing their tour of the facility, Coach Roberts stomped across the field. *Could he have been the one I saw in the locker room?* Frank wondered. *Did he have something to do with Coach Sant'Anna's collapse?*

The team captains passed out assignments. Frank was asked to help manage the equipment for the American team. Joe was assigned to the referee squad. He would keep track of the red cards and yellow cards that referees hold up to indicate fouls and misconduct.

It was a long but exciting work day. At the end of the afternoon, the volunteers were given T-shirts, shorts, and cool blue jackets with the logo of the tournament printed on them. They were also each assigned lockers in the equipment room so they could stash some their uniforms and anything else they didn't want to cart back and forth to the field.

"So, you guys have plans for dinner?" Jacques asked the Hardys as they left the stadium. They were in an old industrial part of the city outskirts that was sprinkled with factories and warehouses.

"I don't care where we eat, as long as it's soon," Joe said. "I'm totally starved."

"There's some good burger places on the Champs," Jacques said. "Even some that'll be familiar to you."

They took the Metro, Paris's subway system, to the Champs-Elysées, the grand avenue in the center of Paris that led to the Arc de Triomphe. Frank and Joe had each bought a Paris Visite card, which gave them discount rides on the Metro and city buses for five days. In a short time they were in a restaurant filled with smells of crispy *pommes frites* and burgers.

"So did you hear all the rumors about Coach Sant'Anna?" Jacques asked the Hardys as they finished ordering. They took their burgers, *pommes frites,* and sodas to a table by the window. There they could see the constant parade of people along the Champs as they talked.

"He didn't just collapse or have a heart attack," Jacques continued, stuffing French fries in his mouth. "They think someone actually attacked him."

Frank and Joe exchanged looks. "Who told you that?" Frank asked, chomping a bite of his burger.

"Everyone's talking about it," Jacques answered. "They're just rumors now, but I hear it's going to be on the television news tonight."

"But who would attack Coach Sant'Anna?" Joe asked.

"And why?" Frank added.

"Well, most of the players think it was Montie Roberts," Jacques told them. Joe coughed as he swallowed a gulp of soda.

"It makes sense, really," Jacques pointed out. "The amateurs from Brazil—Coach Sant'Anna's team— are really great, and the British team's been having problems. Everyone's heard Monster Montie rip into opposing players and coaches."

"Yeah, but there's a difference between threats and actual physical violence," Joe pointed out. "Has he ever really hurt anyone?"

"Only his own players," Jacques said with a chuckle. "I've seen him yank some of them around pretty good."

Frank had a sudden vision of the figure in the locker room with Coach Sant'Anna. In his mind, he superimposed Coach Roberts's face on the shadowy figure. "Hmm . . . his face would fit on the body I saw," he whispered to himself. Then he turned back to Jacques. "I wonder how Coach Sant'Anna is. Have you heard anything about his condition?"

"My contacts say he's still unconscious," Jacques answered.

"Man, that's rough," Joe said, shaking his head. He took a long drink of soda.

"I won't be surprised if they find out that the fireworks incident wasn't an accident either," Jacques said.

"So are there rumors about that, too?" Joe asked. "Does everyone think Montie had his fingers in that?"

"Haven't heard anything so far," Jacques said. "The authorities seem to be holding that case a little closer to the vest, as they say. No one's talking much about it. But if Montie's gone beyond just bullying the opposition . . . ," Jacques said, gazing out the window. "If he's trying to sabotage the whole tournament . . ."

Frank and Joe followed his gaze to the steady stream of characters walking by the window. No one spoke for a minute or two. "Maybe there'll be more about the fireworks incident on the news tonight too," Frank said finally, checking his watch.

"Oh, I forgot to tell you the best part," Jacques said. "My contacts told me that you're going to be famous by the time the newscast is over, Frank."

"Me?" Frank exclaimed.

"You bet," Jacques said. "First, you and Joe got everyone out of the way of the unexploded firework canister; that could have been a lot worse without your heads-up. Then Frank's the one who found Sant'Anna. You are going to be celebrities in Paris!"

"That's all we need," Joe said with a grin.

"Tell me more about Isabelle Genet and her group, Victoire," Frank said. He wanted to change the subject. "Have they ever done anything more dangerous than lobbing tomatoes into people's faces?"

Joe's grin faded. "Good question," he said. "As far as I'm concerned, that group is a prime suspect for the fireworks accident—if it *was* sabotage."

"They've pulled off some minor capers here and there, but nothing really life-threatening that I know of," Jacques answered. "No one knows where their headquarters are. They just sort of materialize for their rallies and protests. I know where Isabelle lives, though. It's in Montmartre." He wrote down her address and drew a simple map to her house. "I'd be glad to run you by there any time. I heard she's organized a demonstration for tomorrow morning at the Conciergerie."

"That's the old prison," Frank said. "Where Marie

Antoinette was held until she went to the guillotine."

"That's it," Jacques said. "It was originally a palace. But from the late fourteenth century to 1914, it was used as a prison and a torture chamber. We Parisians say that the gloomy air inside the structure is filled with the ghosts of Robespierre, Marie Antoinette, and others. Isabelle holds her rallies there often."

"We don't have to report to the stadium until four," Joe said. "Let's go to the demonstration."

"Absolutely," Frank said.

"Good," Jacques agreed. "I'll meet you at ten A.M. outside the Conciergerie. See you then."

Jacques left, and the Hardys followed soon after. Their Metro stop was just four blocks from the apartment where they were staying. It was a quiet neighborhood with lots of leafy trees and winding streets and with very little traffic.

"I can't wait to tell Dad about what happened at the stadium today," Joe said. "I hope he's back at the apartment."

"He's probably already heard about it," Frank said. "I figure the security conference got word before anyone else. But he might not know how much we—"

Frank never heard it coming. Like a flash of fire, a large man flew out from behind the tree. One hefty arm in a bright red sleeve shoved through the air and straight at Frank's stomach.

4 A Clue of Gold

"Ooooshhh!" When Montie Roberts's fist slammed into his stomach, the breathy groan wheezed out of Frank's mouth like air from a stabbed balloon. His eyes squinted shut, but he still saw bolts of electric blue and neon green behind his eyelids. The pain that started in his gut quickly shot through his arms and legs. Before he could catch himself, he dropped to his knees.

"Hey, you maniac!" Joe yelled. He moved fast to confront Coach Roberts.

Frank shook his head until all the colored lights and fuzzy sounds stopped. Then he stood up. Coach Roberts and Joe were sparring under the streetlight. The coach was heavier and his fists were twice the size of Joe's, but Joe was quicker on his feet. He was able to dodge the coach's blows and land a few of his own.

"I'm going to teach you punks a lesson," Coach Roberts snarled, his face as red as his jacket. "You're going to learn to stay out of my way."

Still reeling from the blow to his stomach, Frank gasped for air. He stumbled into the apartment and to Fenton's room. He took a pair of handcuffs out of a small brown bag from his dad's suitcase, stuck them in his pocket, and returned to the sidewalk.

By the time he was back outside, his strength had begun to return. He sidled into the fight and delivered a few well-aimed blows of his own. Frank thought it was like fighting an enraged grizzly.

Frank motioned to Joe to help push the coach over to the dark green wrought-iron fence that bordered the front lawn. The coach put up a huge fight, but both Hardys were too much for him. He staggered back under Joe's steady jabs until his back was against the fence.

Frank's timing was perfect. He remembered the drills his dad had put him through to cuff a perpetrator: left hand, grab the perp's arm tightly and swing it back around; right hand, pull out the handcuffs and slap them against the perp's wrist.

This time it was Coach Roberts who got the surprise. Frank pulled the coach's arm back so that the cuffs closed—and locked—around both his wrist and the long horizontal bar of the wrought-iron fence.

Joe leaned over, bracing his hands against his knees. He sucked in big gulps of air, then stood back up. "You okay?" he asked his brother.

"Yeah," Frank said with a smile. "Just catching my breath."

"Me too," Joe said, nodding. "I'll call the police."

At first Coach Roberts said nothing. He made a few feeble tries at pulling loose, but quickly gave up. He started just to lean against the fence and rub his forehead with his free hand.

"What's going on, Coach?" Frank asked. Every breath reminded him of the blow he'd taken earlier. But Roberts was silent.

Two French policeman arrived quickly, and the Hardys told them what had happened earlier at Le Stade and the ambush Coach Roberts had set up for their return to the apartment. At first Roberts refused to talk, but eventually he broke down.

"I didn't plan this," he said.

"Yeah, right," Joe countered. "You just followed us home and jumped Frank on a whim."

"I mean I didn't plan to attack him," Coach Roberts said. "I followed you here, yes, but just to talk. I recognized Frank when he surprised me in the locker room. That was a setup. I'd gotten a note telling me to come to the locker room for an important scouting report on the Brazilian team. But when I got there, I found Gabriel lying on the floor."

"He was already unconscious when you got there?" Frank asked.

"Yes," Coach Roberts said. "I could tell he'd been attacked. You came in just minutes after I found him, and I panicked. I figured everyone would think I was the one who beat him up." His face started to flush again, and his eyes flashed with anger.

"It was you," he said, pointing to Frank. "You were the one who set me up! Why else would you show up just a minute or two after I did? You must have been the one who'd sent me the note. Which means you must have been the one who beat up Gabriel Sant'Anna."

"You're nuts," Joe said. "My brother would never do anything like that."

"Well, that's what I came here to find out," Coach Roberts said. "I was just going to talk to you," he added, looking at Frank. "But when I saw you, I lost it. You set me up, and you deserved everything you got."

"I didn't set you up, Coach Roberts," Frank said. "And I don't know who did."

"Well, I didn't beat up Gabriel," Coach Roberts insisted, this time to the police. "He's a great coach and a worthy adversary. I prefer to beat him on the field."

"Right now, it doesn't make any difference whether you attacked Coach Sant'Anna or not," one of the officers said. "You *did* attack these gentlemen here, and that's enough for us to take you in."

Assailed by the coach's loud protests, the police bound the coach with their own handcuffs and carted him away.

Frank and Joe watched the police car pull away before walking into their apartment. "Nice move with the handcuffs, bro," Joe said, clapping Frank on the shoulder. "How's your gut?"

"Sore," Frank admitted. "But I'll live." He put his dad's cuffs back in the brown bag and returned them to the suitcase. Then he and Joe went to their room to clean up.

"There's a note from Dad," Joe said as Frank peeled off his T-shirt. "He's going to be really late tonight—says he might not see us till breakfast tomorrow."

Frank emptied the pockets of his khakis. The small gold ball that he'd found near the fireworks compound rolled around the dresser top.

"Hey, look," Joe said as he watched the small charm roll around. "That's not a soccer ball after all. It's kind of got wrinkles on it, and—"

"It's a walnut," Frank said, picking it back up and looking closer. "It's a gold walnut."

"Who'd carry that around?" Joe wondered. "That's pretty weird."

The bed felt good to Frank's sore body. While the rest of him sank down into much-needed rest, his mind still jumped. *Was the fireworks incident really sabotage?* he wondered. *Was the assault on Coach Sant'Anna an unrelated incident by a rival—somebody like Montie Roberts? Or were the two connected somehow? Were they both part of some greater plot to disrupt the tournament—maybe planned by the radicals of Victoire?*

Thursday morning was overcast and surprisingly chilly. Frank pulled on a tan sweater and his khakis. Joe grabbed a blue striped rugby shirt and jeans. Their father was waiting for them with breakfast and the morning English-language tabloid papers.

"So, looks like you guys were busy yesterday," their dad said with a grin. He shoved the newspapers across the table. The headline stories were full of the fireworks mishap at Le Stade and the attack on Coach Sant'Anna. Frank was mentioned in two of the stories.

"Oh, man, did you see this?" Joe asked, and then read aloud from one of the stories. "'Frank Hardy is in Paris as a volunteer for the soccer tournament and, with his brother and father, one of an American family trio of professional and amateur detectives.'"

"Looks like we've been discovered," Fenton said with a crooked smile. "Everyone knows who we are. At least they don't seem to know that I'm in town too. We need to keep that quiet if we can."

The three compared stories about their first day. Fenton conceded that his was a lot quieter than his sons' had been. "You know I can't tell you any of the specifics about what's going on in the conference," he reminded Frank and Joe. "But I can show you some of the stuff we're trying out."

For the next hour, the three Hardys checked out some of the booty that their father had gotten from various security firms. Commercial sponsors and associates of the symposium distributed samples, demos, and prototypes to the people at the conference. Fenton and the others would try out the equipment and report their findings.

Fenton showed his sons sunglasses equipped with hidden digital cameras and amazing handheld devices. Then they tried out surveillance microphone/recorders that looked like small belt-radios with earplugs. "These can pick up conversation fifty yards away," Fenton told them. "And the listening device is a remote; it doesn't have to be connected to the recorder."

Soon the breakfast dishes were pushed aside and the table was covered with cutting-edge inventions and gadgets. At nine o'clock Fenton's unmarked, tinted-windowed car arrived. The three Hardys said their good-byes and exchanged warnings to use caution and keep their eyes open.

At nine-thirty Frank and Joe packed some of

Fenton's surveillance equipment in their backpacks—just in case—grabbed their jackets, and headed for the Conciergerie.

As they walked along the street bordering the Seine, Joe stopped at a computer café. "Something's nagging me about that gold walnut I found," he said. "I want to check something out. I'll only be a few minutes."

While Joe was inside the café, Frank walked over to join the crowds strolling along the famous tree-shaded bookstalls lining the riverbank. He was drawn to one particular stall that specialized in maps. He zeroed in on a large portfolio of antique sailing charts. While he carefully turned the yellowed pages, he felt for a moment as if he were back at home on his boat.

The chill had lifted and the sun peered from around the clouds. It was just enough to warm the busy quai, the embankment where the bookstalls were located. Many people milled along this popular spot, jostling one another as they reached for a book, magazine, or drawing.

Frank held tightly to his spot as individual shoppers wove in and out of the crowd. He took care to cradle the leather portfolio in his arms and keep the old maps safe and untorn. Occasionally he'd feel an elbow dig lightly into his side or a shoulder press against his arm—but he was able to stand firmly.

Finally he checked his watch. It was close to ten o'clock—almost time for the Victoire demonstration. As he closed the portfolio he turned slightly, looking toward the computer café for Joe. He started to nudge his way through the crowd, but his path was suddenly blocked by someone.

For a second he felt almost caged. Adrenaline flooded through him as he realized he was wedged against the side of the bookstall. Then he felt a strange, cold, steely-hard object jammed into his kidney and someone's breath on the back of his neck.

"Do not turn around," someone ordered in heavily French-accented English. "Just keep looking at the nice books, and listen carefully to what I say."

5 Hanging with Marie

"I'm listening," Frank murmured. He didn't know whether the cold metal in his back was an umbrella handle, a comb, a knife, or the barrel of a gun. And he wasn't sure he wanted to know. He dropped the portfolio onto the stack of books displayed at the front of the bookstall and pretended to page through it slowly. And all the while, he listened.

"I know who you are," the voice behind him said. "And I know what you're doing. This will be the only warning you get. Stay out of the situation at Le Stade. It is none of your business. Do as I say if you want the 'American family trio of detectives' to remain intact."

Frank nodded. He hoped to keep the person talking a while longer. Maybe then he could get a clue as to who it was. So he decided to risk a conversation.

"I don't know what you're talking about," he said. "What is it you think we're doing?"

There was no answer from behind, but he still felt something jammed in his back.

"What do you mean by the situation at Le Stade?" Frank said, trying again to get the person to talk. "I still don't know what you're talking about."

Again there was no response. Suddenly Frank felt the object leave his back. The person had left. As quickly as the threat arrived, it was gone, the bruising pain in his back with it. Frank whirled around, scanning the area for clues. He couldn't tell which one of the dozens of people moving away was the one who had delivered the message.

Frank met Joe as he came out of the computer café. When he told his brother what had happened, both looked around the bookstall, hoping to find a clue. But they found nothing. Plus, the person was impossible to find in the crowd of strollers.

"Okay, we're going to have to be very careful from now on," Frank concluded. "Dad was right. We've been totally found out. Anyone keeping up with the news knows who we are."

Frank looked around. He felt edgy as he scanned the crowd. Then he looked back at Joe. "Did you find what you were looking for in the computer café?" he asked.

"Sure did," Joe answered, showing Frank a printout from the computer he'd been using. "It's a biography of Montie Roberts. Something's been nagging me about that gold walnut, and I found out what it was."

Before Frank could read the printout, Joe pulled it back. "Listen to this," he said. "Montie wasn't always a university coach. He had once coached at a boarding school outside of London. That school's arch-rival was another private school with an English walnut in its crest."

Then Joe read directly from the printout. "'Before every game with his rival, Monster Montie's pep talk always ended with his pulling a real walnut from his pocket and placing it on the floor. Then he lifted his size nineteen brogan off the ground and slammed it down on the walnut, crushing it to bits.'"

"That pretty much gets the message across to the team, doesn't it?" Frank said.

"Absolutely," Joe agreed. "When he left that school, the team gave him a golden walnut as a keepsake and good luck charm. The bio says he's carried it ever since."

"Until yesterday," Frank said.

"It's got to be his," Joe said. "There's probably no one else in Paris carrying around a golden walnut."

"So the question is, what was Magnificent Montie doing hanging around the fireworks crew?" Frank wondered.

"You know, if he is behind all this, he must have

sent the guy to threaten you just now," Joe pointed out.

"He swears he was set up," Frank reminded his brother.

"Yeah? Well, that's getting harder to believe, isn't it?" Joe said.

The Hardys hurried on to meet Jacques at the Conciergerie, where the Victoire members were assembling outside a huge Gothic palace with pointed towers. "I can see why Isabelle Genet picked this site for Victoire's protest demonstrations," Joe said. "It's pretty spooky."

Isabelle was already standing on a platform and talking to the small crowd. She had on her camouflage uniform and combat boots, and her red hair looked even brighter in the sunlight. Joe, Frank, and Jacques blended in with the group and then fanned out a little.

Joe listened for a while. Isabelle switched back and forth from French to English, so although Joe wasn't as good at translating as his brother, he still picked up most of what she said. It was pretty much the same speech that she had been giving when he caught the tomato in the face.

While listening, Joe observed the crowd. He tried to pick out the ones who were really members of Victoire. Some were easy to peg. They wore tan T-shirts with VICTOIRE scribbled across them in large purple letters.

As he watched the rest, he noticed a young woman who seemed to be watching *him*. When he caught her eye, she looked startled. Then she turned and disappeared quickly into the growing crowd.

Joe wandered along, watching for her. Finally he saw her again. This time she seemed to be signaling to one of the other Victoire members. She nodded her head toward the building and then back at the man. He nodded back and then disappeared into the crowd.

Joe ducked out of her sight and watched as the woman moved toward the building and crept around the corner. He looked around for Frank or Jacques. He wanted to let them know what was happening, just in case. But he couldn't see either one.

Joe decided he'd better not wait for them, as it might mean losing the opportunity. He cautiously followed the woman around the corner of the Conciergerie. As he walked, Joe remembered the disturbing warning that Frank had been given earlier. He kept his guard up and a healthy distance between himself and the woman he was following.

Joe watched the woman go into the Conciergerie, and after a short wait, he walked through the entrance after her. He found himself in a large vaulted stone chamber that was dimly lit and gloomy. He felt his muscles tense. His senses were on high alert.

He sidled close to the shadowy wall and followed the young woman down a spiral staircase. Downstairs, prison cells with costumed mannequins displayed life as it had once been in the prison and the torture chamber.

The woman suddenly stopped and looked around. Joe ducked back into the shadows, waiting. The woman was standing in front of Marie Antoinette's old cell.

Inside the room were two life-size figures. A mannequin dressed like Marie Antoinette sat in a chair reading. A mannequin dressed as a uniformed guard stood watching. A few other chairs, a cot, and a small writing table filled out the small cell.

Quietly Joe reached into his backpack and took out the long-range microphone/recorder that his dad had gotten at the conference. The Victoire woman paced back and forth until the man she had signaled to earlier arrived.

Joe backed up about thirty yards to a spot where he could still see the two. Then he hoisted himself up to a beam overlooking the cell and the two Victoire conspirators. He turned on the recorder, aimed the mike, and placed the earpiece in his ear.

The two began speaking quietly, but then got into a heated argument. Joe could translate some of the conversation, and two terms he understood very well: "Le Stade" and *"spectateur."*

The Victoire couple left after about twenty

minutes. Joe packed up his gear and swung down from his spy perch.

When he reached up to pull down his backpack, he heard a shuffling noise coming toward him. Before he could turn, he was hit with a crushing blow, and someone's head butted into his side.

"Oooomph!" Joe groaned as he doubled over and crashed onto the stone floor. Fighting down the searing pain, he scrambled back up just in time to see someone grab his backpack and take off.

6 Gimme an M?

Joe ignored the hot pounding pain in his side and chased after the thief. He could hear footsteps. In a flash he realized that the recorder he borrowed from his father was still on. He was able to follow his backpack thief by paying attention to the volume of the footsteps. The quieter they were, the farther away the culprit. "Thanks, Dad!" he whispered, winding through the halls and rooms until he caught up with his attacker.

"Hey!" he yelled at the man just ahead. "Drop that pack!" Yelling made his side hurt all over again, but he had no choice. They had come to a wall, with halls going both right and left. Within moments his attacker turned. Joe recognized him as the Victoire man he'd watched earlier.

The man started to the left, then suddenly ran to the right. But Joe was on to the plan. He cut off the thief and tackled him to the floor. They wrestled for a few minutes, each trying to get the advantage. At first Joe felt like he was in a fight for his life. Then the man seemed to weaken, and Joe was able to pin him.

"Who are you?" Joe demanded. But there was no answer.

"Comment vous appellez-vous?" Joe asked. "What's your name?"

The man struggled a little, but soon gave up completely. And he remained silent. Joe could tell he wasn't going to get the man to talk, but he also knew the stranger had no power left in him to fight. He decided to release his hold and stood up. The man dashed off, leaving Joe's unopened backpack crumpled against the wall.

Joe checked the bag. The man apparently hadn't had time during the chase even to open it. All the items were safe just where Joe had placed them. And the recorder was undamaged.

With a sigh of relief and a moan of pain, Joe walked toward the spiral staircase leading up out of the dungeon.

While Joe was in the Conciergerie, Frank and Jacques mingled in the Victoire demonstration. Frank nudged closer and closer to the front of the rally. At one point in her speech, Isabelle Genet looked right at him, and her mouth twisted into a thin-lipped crooked smile.

"Do you think she recognizes me somehow?" Frank murmured to Jacques. "She looks like she knows who I am." Frank kept watching Isabelle, who was no longer looking at him. "Jacques," Frank said in a low voice. "Jacques?"

Frank looked around, but Jacques wasn't there. He peered over the heads of some of the others at the rally. He could see Jacques at the fringe of the crowd, but decided not to join him. He wanted to keep his eyes on Isabelle. He had an idea for getting her to talk to him and maybe reveal more of her plans.

When the rally ended, Frank closed in on Isabelle. "I remember you," she said to him as he approached. She had a deeper voice when she talked in conversation. It wasn't as shrill as the voice she used when she was marshaling her Victoire troops for battle against progress. Up close she looked a little younger than forty, the age Frank had guessed for her the day before. But she also looked tougher.

"You were at Le Stade yesterday," she continued, "with your friend, tomato-face." She gave him that crooked smile again.

"My brother," Frank corrected her. "And you might be sorry you did that when you hear what I have to say."

"I'm listening," Isabelle said, plopping down onto a bench near the quai.

Frank sat next to her and began his story. "My brother and I believe in what you stand for," he said. "In fact we'd like to organize a group like yours in America. Why don't we go get some coffee and you could give me some tips on how to get started." He pointed to a small café on the bank of the Seine near a bridge.

She looked at him closely, studying him. Then her eyes narrowed, and he had the sudden feeling she could read his mind. Finally her eyes widened again and she spoke. "Hmmmmm," she purred. "How do you Americans say it? Oh, yes . . . NO WAY!" She stood up and strode off, without a backward look.

Frank talked to a few of the other Victoire members, but none of them seemed to be really clear about Isabelle's plans. He checked his watch. It was two-thirty.

"I hope we've got time to eat." Joe was also checking his watch as he walked up to Frank.

"Hey, there you are," Frank said. "I've been wondering what happened to you. You sort of disappeared." He noticed Joe seemed to be limping a little. "You okay?" he asked.

"Yeah," Joe answered. "Just a football head butt in the side, that's all. I'll tell you about it over lunch."

They went to the little café by the bridge and

filled up on soup and sandwiches. Joe told Frank about his adventure in the dungeon of the Conciergerie and played the tape he'd made. "They're definitely talking about the stadium and the spectators," Frank agreed. "We need to get this translated. Do you know what happened to Jacques? He disappeared about the same time you did."

"Nope," Joe answered. "We'll hook up with him at Le Stade."

"Good," Frank said. "Let's stop at the hospital," Frank said. "I want to check up on Coach Sant'Anna." He told Joe about his brief talks with Isabelle Genet and a few of the Victoire conspirators. "I got the feeling she didn't believe me. I wonder if she could have figured out who we are from the news."

"Well, I don't know about you," Joe said, "but these Victoire guys smell like prime suspects to me." He checked his watch. "Come on—let's get to the hospital."

The Hardys took the Metro to the small private hospital where the coach was staying. Coach Sant'Anna had a room to himself on the third floor. As they started down the hall, they saw a guard posted at the coach's door.

"Can you distract him so I can sneak inside the room?" Frank whispered to his brother.

"I've got just the stuff for the job," Joe said with a grin. "Leave it to me."

Frank watched from his vantage point at the end of the hall. Joe sauntered down to where the guard stood and began talking to him. Frank watched as the guard responded by shaking his head. It looked as if Joe and the guard were having language problems, with Joe not understanding a lot of French and the guard not understanding a lot of English.

Then Joe swung his backpack around and reached in to pull out the microphone/recorder. The guard plugged in the earpiece and held the recorder, and Joe disappeared around the far corner. Frank saw the guard nod his head, so he could tell that the guard heard what Joe was saying even though he was out of sight.

When the guard started to wander away in Joe's direction, Frank moved quickly down the hall. The guard disappeared around the corner, and Frank slipped into Coach Sant'Anna's room.

An acrid medicinal smell filled Frank's nose. He walked quietly to the bed and peered down at the patient. The coach's eyes fluttered open, and he gave Frank a weak smile and a nod. He seemed happy to have company.

"Do you remember what happened to you?" Frank asked. The coach nodded his head.

"Can you tell me?" Frank asked.

Coach Sant'Anna shook his head and pointed to his mouth. Then he pointed to a pad and pen on the bedside table. Frank realized that the coach was unable to talk. He handed the paper and pen to him and waited.

The coach scribbled a little on the top page of the pad. But he was interrupted by the shrieking voice from the doorway. *"Non! Non!"* a nurse cried. Frank wheeled around, but she was already gone. *To get the troops, I'll bet,* Frank told himself.

The coach tossed the notepad to Frank and nodded. Frank left the top page intact—for the police to find—and tore out the second page. He jammed it in his pocket, thanked Coach Sant'Anna, and rushed to the door in two long strides.

He could hear people people running in the hall and their excited chatter. He checked the room for another exit, but there was nothing—not even a railing outside the window. The thumping in his chest completely drowned out the scratchy creak of the turning doorknob. Finally the door clicked open and inched toward him.

7 Gimme a W?

Trapped in Coach Sant'Anna's hospital room with no place to hide, Frank decided to take the offensive. He took a deep breath, and as the door opened, he strode toward it.

The door swung open all the way, and the opening was filled with the large body of a police guard. His hand rested on the holster that hung from his hip. The room was dimly lit, but he glowed with the brightness in the hall. He had an odd sort of halo all around his body. Frank couldn't see his face clearly, but he was sure the man wasn't happy.

"*Halte!*" the guard said in a deep loud voice.

Frank stopped moving. "*Pardon, pardon. Je suis Frank Hardy.*"

"Hardy?" the guard repeated, stepping into the

room. He turned slightly, and Frank could see his face better. He was a little flushed, and his eyes narrowed as he scrutinized Frank closely. "You are Frank Hardy?" he asked in English. "The one who discovered this patient at Le Stade?"

"Yes," Frank answered quickly. He talked very fast, hoping to convince the guard to overlook his secret visit. "I'm sorry to have intruded here. I just wanted to see Coach Sant'Anna and make sure he was okay." He gave the guard his biggest, brightest smile.

The guard did not smile back, but he took his hand off his holster. Then he walked over to the bed and spoke a few words to the patient. Frank watched as the coach nodded his head.

The guard returned to Frank, took his arm above the elbow, and firmly walked him to the door. "I know who you are and what you did yesterday," he said. "I also know you were the victim of an attack yourself last night. We are sorry you suffered such an experience in our beautiful city. And we are all grateful for your help. Now you must let us be. Do not trouble yourself any longer. Let us do our job, *s'il vous plâit*—please. You must take off your detective hat now and enjoy Paris. *Merci. Au revoir.* Thank you very much and good-bye."

The guard swiftly hustled Frank out the door. The teen started to say something more, but the guard turned his back and fiddled with the doorknob. Frank could tell the conversation was over, so he walked around the corner. Joe was there, waiting.

"So?" Joe asked. "What happened? How's the coach?"

"Okay, I guess," Frank answered. "He's pretty weak and couldn't talk. But he did give me something." He took out the blank piece of paper he'd ripped from the coach's notepad. "Oh, and he's left-handed."

"Which means . . . ?" Joe asked.

"Well, based on how he was lying, it was his left hand that was closest to that letter on the floor. So he actually could have drawn that *M* with the blue marker."

"You don't believe Montie's story, then?" Joe said. "That he was set up?"

"I'm not ruling anything out yet," Frank declared. "It is definitely possible that someone tried to implicate Montie by knocking out Coach Sant'Anna, writing the incriminating *M*, then calling Montie to the scene to be discovered."

"Don't forget the person who arrived just after you did and slammed the door—probably because he or she saw you. If Montie was set up, that could have been the person who did it . . . and then showed up so they could claim to catch Montie in the act."

"Or maybe to blackmail him," Frank said, "to keep quiet about finding him there if Montie paid him. No question—that's all possible." Frank looked at the paper in his hand. "But it's also possible that Coach Sant'Anna marked out that initial himself. Maybe we'll find an answer in this note."

When they got outside the hospital, Frank walked over to a bench and sat down. He held up the paper to the sun and found what he was looking for. "Cool," he murmured. "Coach Sant'Anna was strong enough to push down on the pen. I had to leave the page he wrote on in the hospital for the police."

"Yeah, you're right," Joe agreed. "It's real evidence; they should have it."

"But he wrote hard enough that it imprinted the next page," Frank said. He took a pencil and gently rubbed the side of the lead against the blank paper. Little by little, white lines appeared in the middle of the pencil lead smudges.

"'Not Mon, W,'" Frank read. The rest of the marks were just scribbles and didn't seem to make sense.

"'Not Mon' could be 'Not Montie,'" Joe guessed. "Or 'Not Money'? Maybe it means 'Not Monday'? What do you think the W means?"

Frank looked at the letters closely. "It might not be a W," he said. "It might be two Vs instead. I thought those were just scribbles at the end, but now I'm not sure. I wish I could make them out. They might tell us whether we've got a W or a double V here."

Frank slowly turned the note around, squinting

his eyes as he stared at the pale white letters. He hoped that looking at it from different angles might help him decipher the extra scribbles. When the note was completely upside down, he remembered something. "Wait a minute!" he said. "The *M* on the floor in the locker room—maybe *that* wasn't an *M*. Maybe it was a *W* or a double *V*."

Ignoring a couple of weird looks from passersby, Frank lay down on his side on the bench in the same position that Coach Sant'Anna had been in when he found him. With the pencil, he marked the letter on the bench the way it was on the locker room floor.

"Hey, you're on to something here," Joe said. "From the coach's viewpoint on the floor, it would have to be a *W*—an *M upside down*."

"Or two *V*s," Frank said, sitting up. He erased the mark he'd made on the bench. "If Coach Sant'Anna wrote it with his left hand, it was definitely not an *M*."

"So what would the *W* be for?" Joe wondered.

"I can't think of anything offhand," Frank said. "But the *V* sure brings something to mind."

"Victoire," Joe said, putting his hand on his bruised side.

"Let's keep this to ourselves for a while," Frank said, "and see what we can find out on our own."

Frank and Joe headed for Le Stade and arrived at about 3:45 P.M. Considering the headlines that

55

morning, their reception wasn't too bad. Some of the local volunteers sneered a little, making cracks about foreigners butting in where they're not needed, and some of the others treated them like minor celebrities. But for most of the people, it was business as usual. Everyone seemed to realize how important it was to get all the kinks out of the procedures before the opening ceremonies that evening.

"Whoa, there he is," Joe said, pointing out Montie Roberts, who was coaching his team on the field.

"I'm not surprised he's here," Frank said. "Unless I press charges for assault, that scene with him last night will be considered just a street fight."

"You're talking about Montie, I'll bet," Jacques said, walking up to the Hardys and following Frank's gaze. "He was bailed out last night. And he's barred from any contact with either of you guys."

"Sounds good to me," Frank said. His mind flashed to Montie's powerful punch.

"Plus he's restricted from leaving the city. That's got to be because of the suspicion that he had something to do with Coach Sant'Anna's assault."

But if we're right about the message Sant'Anna left, Frank thought, *Montie might be innocent after all.*

"When the judge told him he had to stay in Paris," Jacques added, "Montie was his usual self. He told the judge he had no intention of leaving; he had a tournament to win!"

"Sounds like him," Joe said, nodding his head.

Frank felt the gold walnut in his pocket. *But what about the fireworks sabotage?* he thought. *I've got to check this out.*

"Oh, by the way," Jacques said, as if reading Frank's mind. "They're going ahead with the fireworks after all."

"They are?" Joe exclaimed. "So they must have figured out how the accident happened. Maybe it was just a fluke occurrence."

"Hey, guys," Jacques said. "I have a proposal for the two of you." He hesitated a few minutes, then began again. "I didn't really know who you were until I heard the news. I'll bet you're working on both these incidents—the attack on Sant'Anna and the fireworks incident."

"Which might be nothing," Joe reminded him.

"Right," Jacques said. "Well, I want to join up with you. The three of us will make a great team. And if I'm in on the case, I'll be able to beat the other reporters to the story. We solve the case, and I'll have the lead byline in every paper in Paris. And I really can help, too. I'm familiar with the local scene and have had a lot of experience as an investigative reporter. I can cut some corners for you and maybe even open some doors."

"At this point you already know everything we do," Frank said. "So it looks like we're already working together."

"Is your dad in Paris?" Jacques asked. "Is he working on the case too?"

"Actually he might be coming in for the tournament," Joe said. *If Jacques is going to be hanging around,* he thought, *he might run into Dad, so I'd better set it up so it makes sense.*

"Great!" Jacques said. "But for now, it'll be just the three of us—saving Paris from the saboteurs!"

All the final walk-throughs and rehearsals went really well, and the volunteer coordinators finally declared that the crew was ready. During the dinner break, Montie Roberts definitely went out of his way to avoid getting too close to the Hardys. Several people commented to Frank about the fight, but he downplayed the whole thing.

When the specatators started filing in, Frank slipped away from the others and headed for the small compound where the Macri Magnifico employees were setting up the fireworks display. He wanted to ask Sylvio about his computer program and whether it really had been tampered with. But the area was completely roped off, and several guards were posted along the ropes. Frank had to leave without even seeing Sylvio.

Le Stade filled quickly for the opening ceremonies. The spectators had come from all over Europe and South America, and there was a large crowd from the United States to support its team too.

"I'm starting to get pumped," Joe told his brother. They were standing on the sidelines with the rest of the equipment squad volunteers watching a marching band lead the parade of teams onto the field.

"Me too," Frank agreed. "But I wish I'd talked to Sylvio." He couldn't shake the feeling that something wasn't right. He looked around the stands, scanning the exits. All he could see were at least a hundred thousand people yelling, colorful banners waving, groups holding up signs in different languages, and uniformed guards, who were also scanning the crowd.

Down on the field the marching band stood at attention at one end, but a rock band held center stage. The spectators first cheered for their teams as they were introduced. Then they screamed and applauded for the singers, dancers, and musicians that performed. The music roared from the speakers, and a young French singer held her own over the crashing chords.

The field filled up with performers in bright costumes. The music grew louder and the beat more hypnotic. It sounded as if everyone within the walls of Le Stade were dancing and singing and cheering and yelling.

Shadows fell over the stands as the sun glided down to the horizon. Joe's whole body seemed to vibrate with the drumbeats and the rocking crowd. When he heard the first pop from the opposite end of the stadium, he jumped. "Looks like Sylvio and the gang are getting started," he yelled to Frank.

Although his brother was only a few yards away, he didn't seem to hear Joe. "No way he can hear me over this noise," Joe said to himself. The voices in the crowd seemed to blend into one huge roar. Joe heard another pop and then another. Instinctively he looked up to watch for the fireworks explosion. Another noise, however, brought his attention back to Le Stade.

The crowd roar suddenly stopped. Joe's pulse seemed to stop too. For an instant all the sounds seemed muffled, as if someone had stuffed wads of cotton in Joe's ears.

Then the sound charged up again. The crowd's roaring changed to cries and shrieks, punctuated by popping and crackling and hissing. Small explosions lit up Le Stade as the lights in the suspended roof burst with shattering echoes and torrents of glass.

8 Yellow Card Up

Joe realized he'd been holding his breath, so he gasped for air. Then he leaped into action. Security guards materialized from every exit and began shuffling people to safety.

"Now's when the safety-conscious design of this place shows its stuff," Joe said to Frank as they pushed a couple of spectators in wheelchairs through the exit. They went back inside, joining other volunteers to help the evacuation. It went like clockwork.

Emptying the full house was a piece of cake. Joe was used to going out to the concession area of a stadium and winding back and forth along ramps and hairpin turns until he finally got down to the main-floor gates. At Le Stade, every exit—every gate—led directly outside. The spectators were cleared out in under eighteen minutes!

"Whoa—they're still going," Joe said, shielding his head with his arm. Another small explosion rained glass spears down on the field.

"I talked to someone in maintenance," Frank said. "He wasn't interested in saying much about what happened. I'm guessing, though, that the lights are controlled by a computer."

"Yeah, that makes sense," Joe said. "Small explosives must have been planted somewhere up there—not enough to cause a huge explosion—but just enough to shatter the lights."

"And when the computer program kicked in the lights, it detonated the explosives," Frank said.

"Exactly," Joe said.

"One of the guards said that as far as he knew, there were only minor injuries," Joe said.

"That's good," Frank said. "It could have been a lot worse if the evacuation hadn't gone so smoothly."

"They're asking the volunteers to help with the cleanup," Joe told his brother.

"Great," Frank said. "It'll give us a chance to check out the place."

The volunteers inspected all the equipment and put it away. Le Stade was also swarming with its own guards, Paris police, and other official-looking security types.

While everyone was busy, the Hardys were able to sneak away for some serious snooping of their own. Frank headed back to Macri Magnifico's setup, once again trying to talk to Sylvio.

As guards moved over the stands and looked under every seat, Joe went into the locker rooms. They were also full of security people. He picked up a short stack of towels and walked through as if he were on official cleanup duty. He tried to over-hear what was being found, if anything, but the conversations were all in French and so muted that he couldn't pick up much.

He wound back out and, still holding the towels, wandered out to the public parts of Le Stade. Secu-rity people poked around the shops, concession stands, and display areas. In the two restaurants, stadium guards looked under all the tables. Joe noticed something odd about one of the officers. He was dressed in the correct uniform, but his shoes stood out. They weren't the black lace-ups of the other guards; they were combat boots.

Joe followed the man as he moved out of the restaurant, through the kitchen, and into a back hall. Keeping in the shadows and ducking into doorways, Joe kept enough distance between them that the guard was clearly not aware he was being followed.

Finally they reached an unmarked door. The guard used a key—or something else—to open it; Joe couldn't tell from his vantage point. The guard disappeared behind the door, and Joe hurried to follow. After a few seconds, Joe slipped inside.

It was a large room filled with electronic consoles and computer equipment. He could see the guard across the room studying a schematic diagram on the wall. Then the man took out a small video camera and begin filming the diagram and the consoles that filled the room. As the guard backed around, Joe kept out of view. The man circled to the door, turned off the camera, and left.

Joe raced to the wall to look at the schematic. Then he left the room and found another security guard. "I just saw someone walking away from that room with a video camera," Joe said. "He was dressed like you, but he had on combat boots instead of plain black shoes. It looked suspicious to me, so I thought I'd better report it."

The guard's face paled and his eyes narrowed as he looked at Joe. He scanned Joe's volunteer ID.

Joe described the man in the boots and wrote his own name and local telephone number on a sheet of paper. The guard released him, with a warning to keep quiet about what he'd seen.

When Joe returned to the field, he pulled Frank over and told him what happened. "I'm not sure because the schematic was really complex, but I think it had to do with sliding the lower bank of stands under the middle bank when they want to have a larger arena," Joe said. "I'm thinking maybe that's the next sabotage plot. I'd hate to think what might happen if they rolled those stands under with twenty-five thousand people still sitting in them."

"It probably wouldn't work," Frank said. "There's got to be back-up security that keeps the stands from moving if people are in them."

"But the saboteur might not know that," Joe pointed out. They agreed to tell no one else but their dad what Joe had seen—not even Jacques.

"Volunteers, listen up." The volunteer coordinator stepped up on a bench and called them all over. Frank and Joe joined the group.

"I'm sorry to give you bad news," the coordinator said, his expression grim. "The security force at Le Stade has determined that, at this time, continuing with the tournament presents too great a risk to the teams and the spectators." A groan rumbled through the crowd.

"As of this moment, the games are officially postponed until further notice. Please clean out your lockers and take everything to your residences. You will all be notified when it's time to report back for duty. I'm sorry." The coordinator hopped down from the bench and tromped off toward the locker room.

The Hardys decided to check in at the apartment, change clothes, and go out for some dinner. They cleared out their lockers and headed home. When they walked in, they found their dad watching the evening news and stirring some soup on the stove.

"Hey, there you are," Fenton said. "Are you hungry?"

"Maybe we'll have a little soup," Frank said. "We're probably going out later."

"So you guys had another busy day?" Fenton asked, ladling up bowls of beef-and-onion soup. He nodded toward the television set. "I've been watching the news since I got home an hour ago. There are lots of special reports about the stadium and the lights. Someone even said there are rumors about another possible plot."

Joe told his dad about his discovery while the three ate their soup. The television stayed on.

"Look, Frank. There's the guy we saw outside the stadium yesterday," Joe said, watching the special report. "Auguste Bergerac, the local politician who's been thrown out of office."

Frank watched the thin man. He was speaking into a small microphone, just as he had the day before outside Le Stade. He was dressed in a suit and tie, with perfectly combed hair. Around him stood a medium-size crowd, a little larger than the group he'd had in front of the stadium.

"So you two know about Bergerac too," Fenton said, smiling. "The symposium thinks he's the one to watch. Listen to what he's saying."

Fenton had tuned to the BBC London station, so everything was in English. Bergerac's speech was translated instantly.

"Do you now understand what I have been telling you?" Bergerac spoke in loud, low tones, but the translator sounded like a young woman. "Do you see how my warnings have come true?"

To each question, the crowd shouted *"Oui!"* A few raised their fists and shook them in the air.

"Since I was ousted from my former position," the woman translated, "the beloved city of Paris has fallen into violent hands. I am no longer your trusted servant and that is an extreme error in judgment. Ejecting me from office has resulted in an increase of crime in our city, a two-day reign of sabotage at Le Stade."

"It's the same basic message he was spouting yesterday," Joe said.

"Only that was before the so-called two-day reign of sabotage," Frank pointed out.

"Why has the crime increased?" Bergerac asked. "What is missing from the government of Paris, missing from the enforcement of the laws? *I* am missing," Bergerac answered his own question. "My leadership is missing. We need to show the world a promise of security during this international event of such high visibility. We need someone pledged to ensure the safety of all involved."

"And that would be you, right, Auguste?" Fenton talked back to the screen.

"You must join me in telling those in charge of security that we are not satisfied with their efforts,"

Bergerac concluded. "Seek out those responsible for protecting Parisians and our international visitors. Express your displeasure with them for these lapses. Demand that they answer our call for a safe, secure Paris." The crowd erupted into raucous cheering and chants.

"He sure knows how to rally the troops," Fenton said, switching off the set. "Most of the people at the symposium suspect that Bergerac and his henchmen were involved in the incidents at Le Stade. They consider him to be the biggest threat by far to the tournament and the stadium. He apparently will do anything to create an atmosphere that will guarantee his reelection."

Frank and Joe told their dad about everything that happened to them that day and about the evidence and clues they'd gathered. By the time they'd finished, they all realized that each of the three had a different theory as to what was happening—and a different suspect.

"From everything I've heard from the security experts, I'd go with Bergerac," Fenton concluded.

"Well, I'm not convinced that Montie Roberts is completely innocent," Frank said. He might not actually be sabotaging the tournament as some people think. But I can't erase the image of him with Coach Sant'Anna in that locker room."

"My vote's for Victoire," Joe said. "If Coach

Sant'Anna didn't write an *M* for 'Montie' as his clue, then it could be a double *V* for 'Victoire.' That guy really clipped me in the Conciergerie. He wanted my backpack and that tape. The tape itself talks about the stadium and the spectators. They're probably referring to messing with the stands."

"We know that a lot of them wear combat boots, too," Frank said, nodding. "That guard could have been one of them in a stolen security uniform."

"Well, whichever one it is," Fenton cautioned, "we can at least agree that we're playing with some pretty heavy hitters. I'm counting on you two to watch your backs."

"We'll be very careful," Frank assured his dad. "And you, too."

By the time they finished their meal, it was close to ten o'clock. "I've got a tour tomorrow morning— can't tell you where," Fenton said. "But the driver's picking me up at five, so I'm hitting the sack. Remember to be careful." With that, Fenton left the room.

"So what next?" Joe asked his brother. "I'm too wired to go to bed now."

"Me too," Frank said. "We're off duty tomorrow from the tournament. So we'll have all day to chase clues. Tonight let's see a little of Paris!"

"Sounds good," Joe said. "I'll call Jacques. He'll

know some cool places to go. We can meet at the computer café by the bookstalls." Joe gave Jacques a call, and the two boys got ready for their night out.

The Hardys arrived at the café first, so they ordered pizza and sodas. When Jacques came in, there was a flurry of recognition. Several customers waved and called to him. A couple in the corner stood and then fell to one knee with bowed heads, as if Jacques were royalty.

"So you're pretty famous here, huh?" Joe said to Jacques as he joined them at the table.

"I've been known to hack around a little in the past," Jacques said, chuckling. "I put myself through university by hiring out my computer skills. Now I just use the word processor." He looked around quickly and leaned in to whisper to the teens. "There's something I haven't told you two yet."

Jacques spoke in hushed tones. "I'm writing a book," he confessed. "It's a real thriller—all about spies and saboteurs. That's why I'm so hooked on what's happening at Le Stade. And that's why I want to hang with you two. You can be models for my spies!"

"Cool," Joe said. He leaned back until his chair rested on the wall.

"See, we can solve this case together, and then I can use parts of it for my book. You cut me in on everything, and I'll trade my hacking skills. Anything you need to find on a computer, I can probably get for you. We can be a strong team."

"Okay," Frank said. "Sounds good."

The three toasted their partnership with sodas and downed the pizza. Then Jacques took them on a tour of some of his favorite hangouts. By the time the Hardys arrived back at the apartment, they were really feeling the effects of the long day.

The two Hardys were in their beds within minutes of getting in the door. Frank mumbled something about making a list of computer chores for Jacques to handle the next day. As he drifted into sleep, a weird two-toned buzz hammered through his foggy brain.

"Mmmph," Joe muttered. "Phone. You get it."

Frank forced himself into full consciousness and sat up. "Where is it?" he asked, turning on the light. Joe's only response was a deep, long sigh ending in a sort of rumbling snore.

Frank stumbled through the room and out into the hall. The phone was buzzing from a small shelf carved into the wall. He grabbed the receiver and cut off the sound in midbuzz.

"Hello," he said. *"Bonsoir?"*

"Frank Hardy?" a scratchy familiar voice answered in English. "This is Isabelle Genet."

9 The Art of Detecting

"Mademoiselle Genet," Frank said. He shook his head; he knew it was time to be wide-awake. "What can I do for you?"

"I would like to meet with you and your brother," she said. "I have changed my mind since our previous conversation. I would be happy to advise you on how to set up an organization like Victoire in the United States. It is an admirable goal, and I should not have been so abrupt in rejecting your request."

"That's great news, Mademoiselle Genet." Frank's mind had gone from nearly asleep to high alert. "When and where?"

"How about meeting at the Louvre," she suggested. "At the foot of La Victoire de Samothrace, at three o'clock?"

"We'll be there," Frank answered. "And thank you."

"*Au revoir.*" Mademoiselle Genet signed off, and the receiver went dead.

By the time Frank got back to his bed, the sleep curtain was closing on his brain again. He scribbled *three—Louvre—IG* on a notepad on the bedside table and quickly sank into a deep sleep.

Friday morning began with much better weather than Thursday had. All the fog and chilly air were chased away by sunny blue skies. Fenton was long gone by ten, the time Frank and Joe rolled out of their beds.

The unexpected invitation from Isabelle Genet made both Hardys suspicious of a setup. Over breakfast they checked out tourist guides to the Louvre. It wasn't easy trying to use small maps to get a feel for the enormous scope and scale of the famous art museum.

"We're meeting at La Victoire de Samothrace," Frank said. "That's the sculpture of Winged Victory."

"Victoire . . . Victory. I get it," Joe said.

"Remember what Dad told us about the museum?" Frank asked Joe.

"You mean the rumors about the passageways and staircases hidden between the walls?" Joe asked.

"Exactly," Frank said. "This place was a palace

for French kings from 1190 on. So there were escape routes built into it."

"It's been a museum for over two hundred years. Too bad the secret stuff isn't on the map," Joe said. He looked at another guide. "I wonder why she chose the Louvre in the first place? It's one of the most famous places in Paris."

"That's probably why," Frank pointed out. "She's really into high-profile places. She works hard at making sure everyone sees her and knows who she is."

"Could be," Joe said with a smile. "And maybe she's just an art lover."

"Or . . ." Frank paused for a moment before he spoke again. "Remember what Jacques told us? No one really knows where the Victoire headquarters is. Maybe it's near the Louvre, and it's just convenient for her to meet us there."

"Speaking of Jacques, should we call him and let him in on this?"

"We can't," Frank said. "It's too risky. We don't know what Isabelle Genet really has in mind. If she's on the level and we bring someone along unannounced, she might get suspicious. If she's trying to trap *us*, we need to travel light. Adding Jacques to the mix could put us in jeopardy."

"I hear you," Joe said. "And I say we pack up some more of the symposium stuff, just in case."

They went to their dad's room and checked

through the samples of spy gear and surveillance equipment that he had collected so far. They each packed a pair of folding night goggles, and Frank chose a voice alterer.

Then they both grabbed a powerful, twenty-first-century device. "Man, these handhelds are way cool," Joe said, holding one of the black devices in his hand. It looked like a cross between a cell phone and a handheld computer. He checked some of the features.

"Okay, it's a phone, of course," he told Frank. "But look. This clicks on the computer. And you can access the Internet like this." He played with the device for a few more minutes.

"You take photos here," he explained, "and you can store them or download them to another computer."

"How do you set up the GPS?" Frank asked. "The global positioning system."

Joe tried a few buttons. "There. See?" He demonstrated for Frank. "Now it's on, and this toggles it off. Dad said we can locate and track one another *from* anywhere *to* anywhere."

"And it works underwater or underground," Frank added.

"Right," Joe said. "But remember, these are only prototypes. So all the bugs might not be out of them yet. We can't fully depend on them."

"Okay," Frank said, packing his handheld away in his backpack. "Let's go."

They had a few hours before the meeting with Isabelle, so they decided to get in a little sightseeing. They took the Metro to the Arc de Triomphe and walked up the stairs to the observation deck on top for a panoramic view of Paris. Then they walked the Champs-Elysées back toward the Tuilleries, a large park bordering one end of the Louvre complex.

Halfway along the avenue, they stopped for *croque-monsieurs*—a popular French sandwich—and *pommes frites*. Then they continued along the Seine to the Louvre. As planned, they arrived an hour early.

They walked across the vast courtyard, surrounded on three sides by the huge former palace. They stepped into the clear glass pyramid that sat like a pointed spaceship in the middle of the courtyard. It was like walking into the middle of a prism. They bought their entrance tickets and then rode the escalator down to the underground reception area of the museum.

They stood in the large open room under the glass pyramid and surveyed their position. Gift shops, restaurants, and snack bars surrounded them. Steps led from the lobby into different wings specializing in certain periods or types of art. Crowds of people moved from the exhibits to the shops to the food and back to more exhibits.

"This is even bigger than I thought," Joe said.

The Hardys walked into the Denon Wing, which

housed the famous sculpture of Winged Victory. They found the sculpture immediately. The huge headless body seemed about to launch itself from its pedestal and soar out over the large sweeping staircase beyond.

Isabelle hadn't arrived yet, so they wandered through some of the enormous exhibition areas. Occasionally smaller rooms led off the main larger spaces. "We don't have nearly enough time really to go through this wing," Frank said. "Let's just do the best we can."

"Whoa, ahead at two o'clock," Joe said, nudging Frank to look up ahead and to the right.

Frank looked up and saw a young man with a camera around his neck. The man was standing against the wall, scanning the crowd.

Joe stepped behind a column and Frank followed. "That's the Victoire guy I taped yesterday in the Conciergerie," Joe told his brother. "He's the one that jumped me and tried to steal my bag!"

"Isabelle's probably not far behind," Frank said. "I don't think he saw us. Let's wait until he makes a move."

They waited about ten minutes. Joe kept the man in sight as Frank looked in both directions for Isabelle. Finally the man stepped away from the wall and started moving away from the Hardys.

Frank and Joe followed the man at a safe distance. When they saw him pause for a minute, they stopped and looked at a painting on the wall. When he stepped forward again, he turned quickly and ducked through an arch into one of the smaller side rooms.

The Hardys walked quickly toward the room into which the man had disappeared. They stepped inside. The room was a medium-size rectangle, about thirty feet long and twenty feet wide. The bottom half of each wall was paneled with rich mahogany wood. On the upper half of the walls hung magnificent Renaissance oil paintings in elaborately carved gold frames.

Mounted in the middle of the room was a large statue of three larger-than-life-size figures. Only two other people were in the room. They were gazing up at an elaborate mural on the ceiling.

Joe instinctively noted the location of a security camera. The red light on the camera was off. Then he glanced quickly around the room, his gaze stopping briefly on every face. "He's gone," he whispered to Frank. "He came in here, but he didn't go back out. He totally disappeared!"

10 Without a Trace

"The Victoire guy came in, he never went back out, and he's not here," Joe said, scanning the room once. "Poof—gone!" Joe walked along one wall, brushing his hand against the wood paneling. "He must have gone into one of those hidden passages behind the wall. That has to be how he disappeared. Now if we can just find the secret door."

"Watch it," Frank whispered. The Hardys both looked toward the entrance to the room. Under the arch stood a museum guard, looking their way. "Let's go for now," Frank added. "I don't want to stand out. We can come back later."

"If I could just hang out here after hours," Joe whispered as they left the room, "I'd definitely find out where that guy went. Did you notice the camera?"

"It looks as if it's been disabled," Frank noted. "Probably by the Victoires. Come on," Frank said when they were back in the main gallery. "There's Isabelle."

"I've been looking for you," Isabelle said. She had abandoned her camouflage outfit for this meeting and was dressed in jeans and a bulky black turtleneck. "You weren't by La Victoire, as we'd decided."

The Hardys greeted Isabelle. "There are too many distractions," Frank told her. "This museum is excellent." The three strolled through the galleries as they talked.

"Mmmmmm," she said, nodding. "So you want to start a Victoire in America. Do you think you will find enough people to make it a real organization? Where is your home base?"

"We're on the East Coast," Frank said, "but we would want to make it a national organization. How old is Victoire? Did you start it yourself?"

"*Oui,*" she said. "I started Victoire almost one year ago. And it was not easy. It still is not easy. Our anniversary is coming up. It is time to make the world listen."

"We'll help—when we start our own group," Joe said. "Whatever it takes, right? It's worth it for the cause."

"Hmmmm," Isabelle said, stopping to turn toward

Joe. "Do you really mean that? How long will you be in town? We might be able to use you two as allies. We have some plans in mind. Perhaps you'd like to be sworn in as Victoire deputies and help us."

"What have you got in mind?" Frank asked.

"Well . . ." Isabelle paused a moment, then resumed strolling through the gallery. The Hardys fell into step beside her. "Let's just say that we intend to make our mark on this city," she said.

"Now would be a good time," Frank pointed out. "The tournament going on, lots of visitors and tourists here."

"Exactly my thoughts," Isabelle said. "Paris is always a hostess for travelers and sightseers, but now is an even more special time. It is like when we hosted the World Cup a few years ago. Many new people, many new minds to reach for our cause."

"So you're concentrating on Le Stade?" Frank guessed. "Something like the attention-getting events that have already been happening over there?"

Isabelle paused again and this time she studied Frank's face. Again he got the feeling she was reading his mind. And he also knew this was one scary woman. He made himself give her a big grin, and then nodded as if they were coconspirators.

Then it was as if an invisible curtain dropped between them. She seemed to be bored with the conversation and distracted, eager to get away. And when she spoke, she no longer sounded casual and friendly. She used a very formal tone.

"I will think about what we've discussed and get in touch with you if I decide that you can help us," she said.

"Don't forget that we would like *your* help too," Frank said.

"Ah, yes," Isabelle replied, "to start your own organization. Well, we will see. This interview is over for now."

She turned and strode away. Frank noticed that she still wore her combat boots.

"That is one spooky lady," Joe said as they watched her turn a corner.

"I had that same thought a few minutes ago," Frank agreed. "I want to follow her and see what happens next."

"Go for it," Joe said. "I'll hang back here. I want to go back to the room where her henchman vanished. I know I can find the trigger that opens that secret door."

"Check your handheld," Frank said. In an isolated corner, they made sure their watches and handhelds were synchronized. "If we don't hook back up before, I'll meet you at closing time down in the reception area."

"Great," Joe said. "Good luck."

"You, too," Frank said, moving toward the corner where Isabelle had turned.

Joe casually meandered back to the room he had started to navigate earlier. There were a few more people in the smaller room, but the guard had moved on. He checked the security camera and was relieved to see it was still turned off. Joe walked slowly around the room, studying the wood paneling. Each wall had several panels that looked a little less than two feet wide. Each panel had a decoration in the top and bottom corners: a small square of wood.

There's probably a sliding mechanism, he thought. *Maybe one of those small squares in the paneling moves to the side and trips the latch on the other side of the wall.* Joe turned to face the room, as if he were looking at the center statue. Then he reached behind his back with one hand and began running his fingers over the small squares of wood.

Keeping his eye on the other visitors, Joe worked his way slowly around the room. Occasionally he pretended to drop his visitors' guide so he could crouch lower. While one hand picked up the guide, the other checked the bottom corners of the paneling for the secret latch.

When he reached the corner of the room, he stood still for a moment. His hands behind his back, he inched his fingertips along the wall. *Wait a minute,* he thought. His right hand retraced the last square he had touched. *There's something different about this one. It's thicker. It sticks out farther from the wall.*

He pushed at the edge of the small square. Still facing out, his hands behind his back, he tried to see the small square of wood in his mind as he worked. He pushed the edge of the square to the right, then to the left, then to the right again. Nothing.

Then he moved his fingers to the bottom of the square and pushed up. At first it didn't budge. Smiling at a young woman who was leaving the room, he tried to push the square up again. At last he felt the wood give. It slid upward and he heard a quiet click.

The left side of the panel behind him gave way slightly, just enough for him to feel it. For a second he thought he smelled something old and musty. He held his breath, not daring to move. *Okay, it's open,* he thought. *Now what?*

He turned to face the wall and looked down at the panel. It extended from the floor to about halfway up the wall, and the whole left side looked as if it had caved in slightly along the edge. While the left side leaned away slightly, the right side was sticking out a little bit. Suddenly this made sense to Joe. *It revolves,* he thought.

He turned back around. There were only three people in the room with him, and they were all men who looked like they were in their thirties. A guard stood not far away in the main gallery. He was a different guard from the one who'd been there before.

Okay, Joe told himself. *Time to rumble.* He took a deep breath and then he yelled.

"My wallet!" Joe called out. "That man took my wallet!"

The three men in the room with him jumped when he yelled. The guard rushed over to Joe and asked in heavily accented English, "What did you say? What happened?"

"That man!" Joe said loudly. "Did you see him? He ran right by you. Wild, long red hair." Joe ruffled his own hair, and then gestured down his chest. "And a long red beard. Bright red. You couldn't have missed him!"

As he talked Joe led everyone out of the room and into the main gallery.

"But, monsieur, I did not see—," the gallery guard started.

"You all saw him, right?" Joe said to the three men that had been in the room. They looked a little startled when he addressed them; he figured they might not understand English.

"He was not too big," Joe continued, spinning a description of his fake pickpocket, "with a green sweatshirt that had a yellow lightning bolt on it. He knocked into me and stole my wallet," Joe said. "Come on—let's get him, before he robs someone else." He motioned to the three men and the guard to join him. Then he took off through the main gallery, running.

The three men and several others joined Joe in the chase. When he looked around, he saw the guard not far behind, talking into his pocket intercom.

Another guard joined the chase, as well as a few more visitors. Some of the crowd parted to let them through. Some stood still in shock while Joe wove in and out. When they reached the crowded main gallery, Joe slowed down dramatically, and the guards and other chasers zoomed past.

Joe ducked into a side room and waited until the posse he had gathered all ran by. Then he slipped back to the room with the secret panel. When he got there, it was completely empty. *Good—the security camera is still off,* he noted. He raced to the corner and crouched down. With a slight push, the left side of the panel swung back and the right side swung out—just like a revolving door.

Joe slipped through the opening and wrestled his backpack through behind him. He pushed the panel back in place from the other side and took a deep breath.

"Whoa . . . ," he whispered. The air was rank. It smelled like rotting meat. Still resting on his heels, he spun around to face total blackness. "Well, wherever I am, it stinks."

He reached into his backpack and pulled out the night goggles. Through them, the strange area where he was crouched glowed a sci-fi green. He was relieved to see that the ceiling was high above him. He stood and stretched his legs. His eyes began adjusting to the eerie light, and he saw that he was in a narrow corridor between two walls of the old palace.

Joe walked along the secret passageway. He could hear skittering sounds ahead. *Something—or someone—is moving around up there,* Joe thought. Still, he forged ahead.

After about twenty minutes of navigating the corridor, he realized that he was going downhill. The air was cooler and he felt a dampness against his skin. Unfortunately the smell of decay grew stronger. Finally the corridor emptied into a large tunnel that Joe figured would be beneath the old palace.

Joe stopped to get his bearings. It wasn't quite as dark here as it was where he'd started, and he wasn't alone. The walls and floor had changed from old wood to uneven rock. He could hear the clattering nails of creatures as they scurried in the shadows. Above him a couple of bats crossed paths and clung upside down on opposite walls. One stretched his little head up to glare at Joe.

A strange sound in the distance caught Joe's attention. He was concentrating so much on listening to it that he didn't hear the soft footsteps of someone rushing suddenly from the side. Turning quickly, he saw a khaki-sleeved arm raised high in the air. Suddenly it swept down toward Joe's head. A slick, slimy rock slammed into his forehead, and the sudden shock of pain made him lose his balance.

Joe tumbled a few yards. The nauseating sensation of losing consciousness rose in his throat, and as the black closed in, his night goggles showed a dozen beady green eyes . . . watching.

11 GPS Says Yes

While Joe was distracting the guards and visitors in the Louvre gallery, Frank was following Isabelle Genet. He tracked her through another wing and into a snack bar. He hung out in a gift shop nearby so he could keep an eye on her.

As she ate, two people joined her at the table. Frank watched as the three talked continually through their meal. Then, as the waitress brought them coffee refills, Isabelle got a phone call. She left the table to take the call. Frank followed her to the small alcove where she was holding her phone conversation. He watched her from a distance.

After the phone call, Isabelle didn't return to the snack bar. Instead she hurried into one of the large galleries in the Richelieu Wing. Frank left his post and followed her as closely as he could without being seen. In a short time she managed to elude him; he lost her trail.

Frank hurried through several galleries on that floor, but didn't find her again. He checked his watch. "Five o'clock," he mumbled to himself. "One hour until closing."

Frank decided to return to the room where he'd left Joe, but his brother wasn't there. He took out his handheld and activated the GPS. Using the handheld, he was able to follow the trail to Joe. He soon found himself in yet another wing of the sprawling museum. With each step he seemed to be closer to Joe.

Just as he thought he might be close to his brother, Frank reached a sort of dead end. *I don't get this*, he thought. *It says Joe is here. . . .* He looked around, but didn't see Joe anywhere. He went to the lowest level of that wing. The small screen on his handheld said Joe was definitely nearby, but Frank couldn't find him. Every time he took off in a different direction, the GPS would guide him back to the same point. It was as if the GPS were leading him in circles.

"Okay, Joe, where are you?" Frank said under his breath. "Ten minutes to closing."

The crowd began to thin and file toward the exit. *Joe has got to still be in the building*, Frank thought, staring at the little screen. *This thing says so. Unless, of course, this is a faulty prototype. . . .*

Frank fiddled with the handheld, turning it off and on and trying different settings. No matter what he did, the GPS still pinpointed Joe as being right near where he stood.

Frank frowned at the small screen. *Wait a minute,* he thought. *Of course! If he's still registering on this, he's still in the area. And if he's still in the area, but I can't see him, he must be in one of the hidden passageways!*

Frank looked around. Guards were ushering people from the galleries into the reception area. He had to think fast.

If Joe found an entrance to the secret passages between the walls, it was probably in that first room we were in, he reasoned. *The one where the Victoire guy vanished.*

Frank dodged the guards and slipped through the crowds of departing visitors. Finally he reached the room where he had last seen Joe. A guard in the room was asking a few people to move on downstairs.

I've got to get out of sight, Frank thought, his mind moving quickly.

Staying out of the guard's line of vision, he ducked into a restroom. The room was empty, and there was no security camera. Frank searched the room quickly for a hiding spot and found a storage closet in the back wall. *Perfect.* He took the lockpick from his pocket and opened the door. Once inside, he lit his penlight, hoisted himself up onto the top shelf, and tucked himself in behind a stack of paper towel packages.

Get comfortable, he told himself as he reached down to the lock and turned the bolt from the inside. *You'll probably have to hide out here for at least an hour while the place is cleared and the guards make their rounds.*

Frank was right. He heard several people wander in and out through the next sixty minutes. Several times, someone turned the knob of the storage closet, but only one person actually unlocked it and looked inside. Frank snuffed his penlight and held his breath. It worked; the guard closed the door and locked it without finding Frank.

Between interruptions, Frank bided his time with his handheld, surfing the Net. First he checked his own e-mail. He had a few notes from friends back in Bayport, and he answered them quickly. Then he searched for a game to play, but he discovered that his mind was so jumpy he couldn't concentrate on it.

He surfed to the Web site of one of his favorite English-language newspapers in France. Scanning the headlines and lead stories, he found out that not much progress had been made on solving any of the incidents at Le Stade.

He also discovered that the authorities had determined the exploding light incident was definitely an act of sabotage. A small article on Coach Sant'Anna stated that he was continuing to improve. *At last*, Frank thought. *Some good news.*

After he skimmed the newspaper, he decided to look up some of the articles that Jacques had published. He fed several possible keywords into the search engine: Jacques's name, the names of some of the papers and magazines he had written for, and a few topics he had researched for stories. But none of Frank's guesses were right. No articles by Jacques Ravel came up.

Then Frank checked the last five years of graduation lists from the Sorbonne, the university Jacques said he'd attended. There was no record of a student with his name.

Frank realized it had been a while since anyone had stopped in to check the room. He looked at his watch. It was seven twenty.

Looks like the closing-time checks are over, he thought. *Now all I have to do is stay ahead of their regular rounds.*

Frank cautiously unlocked the closet and pulled himself out of his hiding place. He flexed his legs a few times before quietly relocking the door. He crossed the restroom, inched open the door, and peered outside.

It was very quiet. Carefully Frank moved into

the hall. Dodging a couple of guards lost in conversation, he took a quick but safe route back to the small room with the elegant wood paneling.

The room was empty. Frank secretly inspected the walls and jumped to the same conclusion: A hidden latch was connected to one of the small wood squares.

After a few unsuccessful attempts, Frank finally found the square that slid up and tripped the latch behind the wall. As soon as the panel began to give, Frank gave it a strong push. The door creaked open. He moved swiftly through the narrow opening and closed the secret revolving panel behind him.

Frank pulled on his night goggles and surveyed the same greenish scene that Joe had earlier. He also smelled the same disgusting stench. But he had an advantage his brother hadn't had. Frank switched on the GPS and discovered instantly that Joe was somewhere to his left.

"Joe?" Frank called out in a loud whisper. "Joe? Where are you?" He hurried along the corridor.

Frank felt a jolt in the pit of his stomach. It was like a chuck of ice milling around inside of him, freezing and burning at the same time. *Something's wrong*, he thought. "Joe, where are you?"

He glanced back and forth from the floor to the GPS screen. Following the trail forged by centuries of people—including his brother—Frank wound down to the cool, damp tunnel. A bat squealed past his head, and the stink of rodents and mold filled his nose.

Frank took in the green scene directly ahead. He spotted Joe lying on the damp floor of the tunnel. His eyes were closed, and his chest was barely moving. Riding the slow, shallow rising of his chest were two large rats.

12 Breakaway to Danger

Frank ran toward Joe, swinging his backpack and yelling. The two rats on Joe's chest scampered off his body and into the shadowy crevice in the tunnel wall.

"Joe!" Frank yelled, feeling his brother's pulse. "Joe! Can you hear me?"

Joe shook his head from side to side. "Oogh. What's that gross smell?" he muttered.

"Probably the rats who were just sniffing around your chin," Frank answered.

Joe sat up quickly, brushing rat hairs off his chest. Then he groaned. "Yikes, my head! What happened?" He felt the large bump on the side of his head. "Hang on. . . . I remember. Someone in a khaki jacket or shirt came flying out of nowhere

96

and decked me." With some help from Frank, he slowly got to his feet. "Man, my head is pounding."

"Come on," Frank urged. "We've got to get out of here and have someone take a look at you." He looked around, then peeled off the night goggles. "There's light coming from down there," he said, pointing. "Maybe that's a way out of here."

They headed for what Frank hoped was an exit. He discovered that the light was seeping through a massive ancient door. A rusty iron bar lay on the ground, and the door had been pulled open about a foot and a half.

"This must have been here for centuries," Frank noted, poking at the wood. "It's solid. Looks like someone's already done the hardest work for us."

"Yeah—the guy I was tailing, I'll bet," Joe said, hauling the door a bit farther across the rock floor. "Let's go." He and Frank—and a half dozen large rats—sidled through the narrow opening. They were finally outside.

Joe stood and inhaled as much fresh air as he could take without hyperventilating. His sore head throbbed. It took several minutes before the smell of the fresh air began to erase the stink of decay that had filled his nose. With each breath he began to feel better.

"Let's get out of here," Frank said. "I want to get you to a doctor." He checked his watch. "It's after eight thirty. Let's go to the hospital."

"No, it's okay," Joe said. "I'm feeling all right now. I just had to get out of that place. I thought I was going to lose it in there a couple of times." He felt the side of his head. "Doesn't hurt as much," he added. "I'm not feeling dizzy or anything. It was just a bump. I'll let you know if I need help."

Joe looked around. It was dark, but there was a full moon. The sky was full of stars above where they were standing, but to the right was the soft pinkish-white glow of electric lights.

They were on a grassy embankment in what felt like a very isolated area. Joe looked back at the door they'd just come through. Vines and grasses almost shielded it from view. If you were passing by and didn't see the rat waddling through the opening, you'd probably not notice the door at all.

He turned around. "That has to be the city over there," Joe said, pointing to the rosy glow in the sky. He took a few steps up the embankment. "Hey, look at this," he called back. "I think it's the Seine— or maybe a canal leading to the river."

"Yeah . . . it's got to be," Frank realized. "If you're setting up an escape route from a palace, you've got to include a path to the river."

The Hardys began walking along the bank toward the city lights. While they walked, Frank told Joe about losing Isabelle in the crowd and hiding out in the storage closet. "One of the first things I want to do when we get back to the apartment is call Jacques," Frank said. "He lied to us about his degree and being a published investigative reporter. I'm going to find out why."

Their path curved with the flow of the water. As they rounded the bend, Joe grabbed his brother's arm. "Hey, check that out," he said in a hushed voice.

Nestled in a secluded cove was a small houseboat with a large purple V painted on the hull. "Victoire," Frank murmured.

"So this is where the Victoire guy was headed," Joe guessed.

"This might even be the private meeting place Isabelle uses," Frank pointed out. "Jacques says no one's been able to find the group's headquarters."

"It doesn't look like anyone's around," Joe said. The inside of the houseboat was dark.

"Let's check it out," Frank said, leading the way down the embankment to the cove.

Armed with penlights and lockpicks, the Hardys poked around in drawers and closets. "If we could just find something . . . ," Joe said from the galley. He scanned his light beam around the narrow pantry. "Anything that tells us that Victoire has been targeting Le Stade."

"Quiet a minute," Frank said. He stopped looking through the writing desk in the small sleeping quarters. "I heard something."

The Hardys stood very still. Both strained to hear

the slightest noise. At first Frank heard nothing but water lapping the hull. Then through the open window rippled the unmistakable laugh of Isabelle Genet.

Frank and Joe quickly cut off their lights. "Hide!" Frank said. He watched Joe dive under a jumbled pile of tarpaulins in a dark corner of the galley.

Frank felt trapped in the tiny sleeping quarters. He could feel the boat give as Isabelle and someone else boarded. He quickly scanned the room for a hiding place but he couldn't find one.

When he saw Isabelle's combat boots on the steps, he knew he had only one choice. He scrambled up over the desk and wriggled out of the window above it. Then he crawled to the inflated raft lying upside down on the back deck and tucked himself under it. The adrenaline shot through his body at lightning speed. His heart was pumping so fast and hard, it made the raft bounce.

Finally he calmed down some. The pulse in his temples quieted, and he could hear what the Victoires were saying. They spoke in French, but he understood most of it.

"Are you sure no one saw you use the secret panel?" Isabelle asked the man with her. "Those Americans were in the museum. I don't like them; they're too curious. And it seems our little warning at the bookstall didn't work."

"No one saw me," her henchman said. "And I fixed the camera, as usual."

"Good," Isabelle said. Frank heard the refrigerator door open. He held his breath as he pictured Joe under the tarps in the galley.

"Did someone beat us to Le Stade?" asked Isabelle's henchman. "Was it an accident that the lights were smashed, or did someone else rob us of our place in the headlines?"

"That we must find out," Isabelle said. "We are working on our plans to bring about destruction at Le Stade. We cannot let others upstage us."

"I say it was no accident," the henchman claimed. "I say we have a rival saboteur, and this will not be good for Victoire and our cause."

"Perhaps we will find out from our friend," Isabelle said. "He must have a reason for wanting a meeting. Cast off, Gaston. It is time to go."

Frank felt a cold ripple down his spine. He heard the words "cast off" echo through his mind. He visualized the boat and the precarious hiding places he and Joe had found. He knew there was no way they could get off the boat now without being discovered. He sent a mental message to his brother. *Stay low. We'll have to ride this one out.*

The boat chugged along at idle speed for a while, then it turned and revved up. Frank figured the boat had left a canal and then turned into the Seine.

They continued to move along the water. Frank

didn't dare turn on his light to check his watch. At last the boat slowed, and he felt a bump. He guessed they had touched against a pier.

"Tie it off quickly," he heard Isabelle say. "I am eager to meet with Monsieur Bergerac."

From under the raft, Frank heard and felt boots clattering across the deck. The boat dipped as Isabelle and Gaston debarked. Their footsteps moved farther and farther away.

Finally, stillness. Frank heard nothing but a nightbird singing and the breeze through the trees. *No time to waste, he thought.*

An inch at a time, he pushed up the edge of the raft and scanned the deck. The houseboat looked like it had when he'd first seen it: dark and uninhabited.

He pushed the raft back completely and slid out from under it. He then pulled himself up to a crouch and looked around. The full moon was so bright that he could clearly see the landscape. It looked as if they were somewhere in the countryside surrounding Paris. They were docked at the foot of a vast lawn leading up to an enormous chateau.

"Frank," Joe whispered from inside the sleeping quarters. "Are you out there?"

"Yeah," Frank said. "Is the boat clear?"

"Yep, they're gone," Joe answered. "Did you hear Isabelle's comment about warning us at the book-stall?"

"I sure did." Frank stood and flexed his arms and

legs. "And now they're meeting with Bergerac."

"Probably our buddy Auguste, don't you think?" Joe said.

"Let's go find out," Frank answered.

The Hardys stepped off the boat and hurried along the pier to the soft green grass of Monsieur Bergerac's country estate. "Watch for guards," Frank warned as they neared the chateau.

As the Hardys got closer to the corner of the building, they heard voices. Frank and Joe both ducked into a tall, unclipped hedge. From there they were able to hear most of the conversation.

"May we speak freely here?" Isabelle asked.

"You may," a deep male voice answered. "Except for my personal bodyguard, my staff has the evening off. I wanted our meeting to be private."

Frank and Joe looked at each other and nodded. It was definitely the voice of Auguste Bergerac.

"Were you responsible for sabotaging the lights at Le Stade?" asked the man with Isabelle.

"I will ask the questions, Gaston," Isabelle said. "Monsieur Bergerac, why have you invited me?"

"Call me Auguste, mademoiselle, *s'il vous plâit*. I am proposing that we combine our efforts. That my network of support and Victoire work together and double our influence."

"Aaaaahh. Well, I don't know," Isabelle responded. The Hardys heard several clinking sounds, like ice being dropped into glasses.

"Think about it," Bergerac urged. "You have yet to make a real mark in Paris. You have yet to command the respect you deserve. If you join with me, your cause will receive a much wider audience."

"That might be true, Auguste," Isabelle began, "but—"

"We do not need you," Gaston blurted out. "We have great plans for achieving the respect you mention. And we will do it on our own!"

"Gaston!" Isabelle ordered. "Enough. Take a walk. Now!"

The Hardys heard grumbling noises, then something that sounded like a glass being slammed down onto a counter or table. They ducked back as they saw a man stomp around the corner and off toward a small building with a fenced pen off to its side.

"As I was saying," Auguste explained, "now is the ideal time for your team and mine to come together. We have prime leverage with this world invitational tournament—many extra visitors to Paris, many opportunities to ensure that the world understands the seriousness of our intentions."

The conversation was interrupted by a sudden ferocious barking. Joe could tell there were at least two dogs, maybe more. The barking and growling escalated to a threatening, terrifying din.

"He has gone to the pen," Bergerac said. "Get him away. He's arousing the dogs."

Another man strode around the corner and off

toward the direction Gaston had taken. "That must be Bergerac's bodyguard," Frank whispered to Joe.

"And it sounds like Gaston has bothered the guard dogs," Joe responded.

The Hardys could no longer hear Bergerac or Isabelle talking over the intense noise from the dogs. The frenetic barking continued in spite of the hollers of Bergerac's bodyguard.

"We might need to find an escape hatch." Joe looked around as he spoke. "We'll never make it to the trees," he said, gesturing to the small woods along the side of the estate.

"If we need to, let's head for the garage," Frank said, nodding toward a large building about fifty yards away.

"I say we head there now," Joe suggested. "Sort of a preemptive escape." He nodded toward Gaston, who was running back toward the chateau. The sound of the dogs had reached a frantic pitch. They sounded like wild animals about to begin a hunt.

"Get inside, Isabelle," Gaston yelled as he raced out of sight around the corner. "We think there are trespassers on the grounds. He's letting the dogs loose."

"That's it," Joe said. "We're out of here. Now!" He and Frank stepped from behind the hedge and streaked away from the house.

The bump on Joe's head throbbed as his legs pounded the ground. He looked around only once, but it was enough. Behind him, taking long, undulating strides, were two huge dogs. Their tongues hung out between pointed teeth, and their eyes were focused right on the teenagers.

Joe felt like prey.

13 And Then There Were Two

Joe raced toward the garage. Frank was not far behind and unfortunately neither were the dogs. The garage had five large doors, all of them locked.

Joe raced around the side of the building and found a small door at the back. He pushed at it, but it wouldn't budge. "No time for the picks," Frank said, running up to join his brother.

"Right!" Joe agreed. The Hardys braced themselves, side by side, their shoulders bowed toward the door. "One . . . two . . . three!" Joe yelled. They ran at the door together, and with a grinding screech, it burst in, tearing the lock from the doorjamb.

Once inside the garage, they shoved the broken door back up against the entry. "This'll buy us a little time," Frank said. He quickly assessed the huge building. A security light shone from the ceiling. Six antique cars were lined up perfectly. On the side wall there was a door that opened to a smaller room. Above that room was a loft storage area.

"Come on," Frank said, leading Joe to the small room. It looked like an office. He reached in his pack and took out an old blue baseball cap. He rubbed it over his head and face, and then over Joe's. Then he scraped it across the floor leading to the small office and threw it behind the desk.

"Grab that box," he said, pointing to a car-repair tool kit on a nearby table. Then they scrambled up the loft ladder.

"Is this going to work?" Joe asked.

"Not for long, probably," Frank said. "But maybe long enough. Check out the tool kit."

As they looked in the kit, they heard the dogs approach the garage. The barking stopped for a few seconds. "They're sniffing for the trail," Joe said. He and Frank planned their strategy.

The dogs suddenly burst into the garage, flattening the broken door with their long muscular legs. They sniffed the floor, heading for the small office. Frank gestured to Joe to be ready.

The dogs followed the trail into the office and to Frank's hat behind the desk. As soon as they were inside the small room, the Hardys dropped down from the loft, armed with tools from the kit, just in case. Joe slammed the door shut, closing the dogs inside the office. Frank got a chair from the corner of the garage and jammed it against the doorknob. Inside, they could hear the dogs tearing into Frank's hat.

"Okay," Joe said, "Let's get out of here."

As Frank and Joe were racing out of the garage they heard one of the larger doors open. "Let's get to the woods," Joe whispered to Frank. They tore across the grounds behind the garage, jumped the metal fence, and bolted for the safety of the trees in the woods surrounding the estate.

The Hardys continued through the woods and finally reached the road. Once there, Joe turned on his GPS device. He punched in *Paris*, and the GPS told them they were eighteen miles from town. Then it drew a little map, showing them which direction to take.

"Come on, let's start hiking," Joe said. "The GPS says this is a pretty direct route. Some cars are bound to come along."

Only fifteen minutes passed before a farmer with a truckful of produce picked them up. They were at their Metro stop in a half hour, and back in their apartment before midnight.

"I can't wait to tell Dad about Isabelle and Bergerac," Frank said as Joe unlocked the door. "I'm not sure which authorities we need to contact here—the local police, or someone higher up. Dad should know exactly who."

"Well, we definitely have to get in touch with someone about it," Joe said.

"Before either Victoire or Bergerac pull off something else," Frank added.

"Auguste and Isabelle—what a creepy combo," Joe said. "Dad," he called as they walked to their bedroom. "We're back, and wait'll you hear what happened."

"Dad?" Frank echoed. "Isn't he home?" He turned to Frank, then continued into Fenton's room.

He wasn't there. And there was no note anywhere in the apartment. Frank couldn't chase away the idea that something wasn't right. "What do you think?" he asked Joe.

"Seems weird," Joe answered. "But with this conference, he could be doing any number of things. Maybe there's some kind of investigative field trip or something—a kind of top-level stakeout."

"Yeah," Frank said. "Could be. But I think it's weird too." He checked the phone messages. "Nothing," he whispered to Joe as he listened. "One from Jacques. He's been trying to reach us." He listened a little longer. "Nothing from Dad so far."

"That reminds me," Joe said. "When are we going to tell Jacques we know he's been lying to us?"

"Tomorrow morning, I—" Frank held up his hand as he listened to the next phone message. "Hold it." He felt his stomach rise into his throat.

"What is it?" Joe asked.

110

"It was a message for Dad from one of his friends at the symposium," Frank said, first hanging up, then dialing. "Dad never showed up this morning. His friend hasn't seen him all day."

He got an answer on the second ring. It was the same man who had left the phone message. Frank asked whether his dad had shown up for any of the meetings later that day. Joe could tell from his brother's face that the news wasn't good. Finally Frank sort of half smiled and hung up.

"What?" Joe asked.

"Well, this guy says not to worry—*yet*. Dad never showed. But the guy says not to contact any of the authorities, that the people in the symposium are already looking into it. He also said that Dad and another guy are working on an actual case to present the final day of the conference. So they think that's probably where he's been."

Joe took a deep breath. "Hey, these guys are masters, right?" Joe said.

"Including Dad."

"Including Dad," Joe repeated. "They're the most qualified to solve this case." Both were lost in their own thoughts for a few minutes.

"So what do you think?" Joe finally said. "Do we worry or not?"

"Not," Frank said, going to his computer. "We're no good to Dad unless we're on top of our game. That means we need all of our pistons firing. *We* just might be the best people on the case."

Frank searched their e-mail in case Fenton had contacted him from another computer. "We got something," he said. "And it's from Dad."

Joe came over to the desk and leaned over his brother's shoulder to see the screen. "'See you tomorrow,'" Joe read. "'I'll be tied up all night.'"

"I don't like the way that sounds," Joe said.

"Agreed," Frank said in a hushed voice. They were quiet as they finally slipped into their beds. Joe fell asleep quickly, but had bad dreams about his father being tied up.

Saturday morning, the first buzz of the phone woke Joe out of a restless sleep. He was very jittery—more than ready to move on the case.

By the time he hung up, Frank had already showered and was getting dressed. "It was the volunteer coordinator," Joe told his brother. "The tournament's back on. We're to report to Le Stade tomorrow morning at nine o'clock."

"That's not a good idea," Frank said. "More 'accidents' are being planned—we both know it."

"How come you didn't mention what we know about Isabelle and Bergerac to the security conference guy when you talked to him last night?"

"Because right now, it's our word against theirs," Frank said. "All we have now is an overheard conversation—in French—about how they might join forces to bring their cause to the international public, plus a garbled tape by someone they can say isn't even connected to them. They'd be able to get us for breaking and entering on the boat, trespassing on Bergerac's property, and breaking the garage door—at least."

"Bergerac was pretty clear about being into sabotaging the stadium or the tournament or both," Joe said. "Do we pin him for what's happened so far? How about the fireworks incident?"

"Probably," Frank said. "I'd like to talk to Sylvio again. For now, though, let's say yes."

"If blowing up the lights was an act of sabotage, we know it wasn't Victoire," Joe said. "Isabelle was so mad about someone beating her to the punch."

"For now, I'd guess Bergerac for that, too," Frank said. "He never answered when they asked him about it."

"What about the attack on Coach Sant'Anna?" Joe asked. "Still thinking Monster Montie?"

"I don't know," Frank said. "I thought it was Montie for a while. But now that we know that Victoire is really stepping up their activity, I wouldn't be surprised if the message Coach Sant'Anna left on the floor was a couple of Vs for Victoire. He's another one I'd like to talk to again. Maybe by now he can tell us what he meant."

"We need proof," Joe agreed. "But first we have to check on Dad. We've got to know he's okay."

"You don't trust the e-mail message?"

"We both know anyone can send one of those," Joe said. "And if they use Dad's computer . . ."

"The return address would be Dad's." Frank finished his brother's thought. "It would look as if it really did come from Dad."

"Hey, anybody home?" The Hardys heard Jacques's voice coming from the front door.

"Let's keep what we've learned quiet," Frank cautioned Joe as they walked to the door.

"And let's say nothing about Dad," Joe added.

Jacques bustled in with sacks of food—sausage rolls, orange juice, and sweet pastries from the patisserie around the corner.

While they ate the three talked about the tournament starting up again. Then, out of the blue, Frank startled Jacques by telling him they found out he'd lied to them.

"Hah!" he said with a grin. "You kids *are* good!" Then his face flushed and he apologized. "I'm really sorry," he said. "I was afraid to tell you the truth. I was sure you wouldn't have anything to do with me. I am an amateur detective myself," he explained. "That is, I *want* to be one."

"That's your story now," Joe said. "How do we know you're not lying again?" Joe asked. He drank his juice in one gulp. He hadn't realized how hungry he was.

"I am not," Jacques said. "I promise this is the truth. When I found out who you two were, I saw a golden opportunity. I'm embarrassed to tell you this, but I wanted to learn some of your tricks. I can see by your faces that lying was a mistake. Let me make it up to you. Let me continue to help you with this case, and I'll be able to prove my good intentions."

"Okay, Jacques," Frank said. "One of my jobs for today was to interview Montie Roberts. Why don't you take that one. Find out where he was just before he came to the locker room. Get all the information you can about the message he says he got that told him to show up there in the first place—how it arrived, who he thinks sent it to him. Oh, and ask him if he's noticed anything missing." Frank could feel the golden walnut in his pocket.

"You've found something. I can tell," Jacques said. "What is it?"

"Just find out what you can," Frank said. "We'll call you later and set up a meeting."

"You've given me a tough assignment," Jacques said. "Trying to get Monster Montie to talk will be a true test. I'll pass it with flying colors." They finished their breakfast and Jacques left.

"Okay, what was that all about?" Joe asked when the Hardys were alone again. "I don't remember you saying anything about talking to Montie."

"I just wanted to get Jacques out of our hair for a while," Frank admitted. "I figured that would keep him busy, and wouldn't really affect our case one way or the other. Plus, it's a good way to find out if he's telling the truth this time."

"Okay, boss," Joe said with a grin. "So what's *our* assignment?"

"I'm going to retrace Dad's route from yesterday morning," Frank said. "Check with his driver, see if anyone along the way saw anything. I want to know if he was diverted from his route, or if he actually never intended to show up at the symposium."

"That's the only part that really bothers me," Joe said. "If this was something he'd planned, he would have told *somebody*. I get that he might not have been able to tell us, but someone at the conference should have known."

"I know," Frank said. "And I agree."

"I'll stake out Isabelle's place," Joe said. He pulled out the map and address that Jacques had given them Wednesday. They synchronized their handhelds and agreed to check in with each other every hour.

By about noon Joe was in the Montmartre district of Paris. A cluster of neighborhoods historically populated with artists, flea markets, and clubs, Montmartre was laid out on a series of steep hills. Joe followed his crude map and finally found Isabelle's garden apartment on a secluded street.

The apartment was half above street level and half below. Joe could look down into the apartment through the windows just above the sidewalk. He saw no one inside, so he climbed over a wrought-iron fence and scurried along the side to the back.

Cautiously he let himself in. The small apartment was dusty and dark. He crept from room to room. They were all empty. The bedroom was off to the side and was separated from the dining room by a heavy curtain that had been strung across the opening. He peered around the curtain. The coast was clear.

As he stepped around the heavy drape, the brass rings at the top of the curtain moved along an iron rod. The sound of scraping metal was answered with a more animal-like sound; a long, low moan filtered through the closet door.

Joe dropped his backpack, picked up a heavy candlestick, and stepped to the closet. Holding the candlestick high above his head, he flung open the door.

14 Buried with the Bones

Joe waited behind the door for just a few seconds. Nothing happened. He peeked around the door and saw a few clothes on spindly wire hangers hanging on a rod. On the floor of the closet was a large wooden trunk with leather straps.

Another moan caused him to spring into action. It came from the trunk—and it sounded like a human cry.

Joe dropped the candlestick, undid the leather straps, and pulled up the lid. Stuffed inside the trunk was Isabelle Genet, handcuffed and gagged. Her eyelids fluttered as the light washed over her face.

"Don't worry," Joe murmured. "You'll be okay." At that point, he didn't know whether he believed what he was saying or not.

Gently he lifted her out of the trunk and laid her on the bed. He removed the gag, but she said nothing. Her eyelids kept fluttering. They didn't stay open for more than an instant at a time. Rummaging through his picks, he found one that worked on the handcuffs. Once he got them off, he rubbed her wrists for a moment and then clocked a weak pulse.

Joe phoned for an ambulance and watched over Isabelle until it arrived. The paramedics checked her out and said a few words to Joe, but he didn't understand them. He could tell by their grim faces, though, that her condition was not good. She didn't speak.

The medics slipped a couple of IVs into Isabelle's arm and hustled her away. Joe got the name of the hospital she'd be in, and thanked them. As they left, one of them turned back to Joe and spoke in halting English. "It is good," she said. "It is good you called. It is good timing."

Joe poked around the apartment a little while but found nothing of any value to the case. *If people know where she lives*, he reasoned, *she's too smart to leave anything incriminating around here*. He left the apartment and called his brother on the handheld. Joe told Frank what had happened, and they agreed to meet immediately at the computer café.

Joe got there first and ordered a soda. Frank arrived a half hour later.

"Sorry," Frank said. "I made another stop."

"Have you found out anything about Dad?" Joe asked. "Finding Isabelle stuffed in that trunk really threw me. These guys—whoever they are—play rough. We need to find Dad."

"I know," Frank agreed. "But I ran into a total dead end this morning. So after you called, I stopped at Jacques's. We know from everything we heard last night that Victoire had nothing to do with the fireworks sabotage or the exploding lights. The only thing they admitted to was plotting something involving the stands. So someone else must be responsible for the rest."

"Right," Joe said, listening intently to his brother. "The fireworks and night lighting both involved computer-controlled systems. The Victoires are such throwbacks, they're not going to be computer experts. They're so antitechnology they're probably not all that tech savvy."

"So who do we know who *is* a superhacker?" Frank asked. "He's also a liar, but the part about being a computer genius is true, because everyone who hangs out here says so."

"Yeah, but Jacques isn't the only superhacker in Paris," Joe pointed out. "Or liar. There's nothing that connects him with any of this."

"That's what I told myself too," Frank said. "So I stopped by just to get his help. I figured we could have him crank up his computer and hack into the

Macri Magnifico database and also into Le Stade's lighting program. I wanted to see if he could track the sabotage hacker." Frank's words were coming fast now. Joe wanted him to cut to the chase, but he knew better than to try to push his brother.

"So I proposed the deal to Jacques," Frank said, "and I was totally surprised by his reaction."

"What do you mean?"

"Well, I figured he's going to be really excited, right?" Frank said. "We're asking him to be involved in one of the most crucial parts of the case—to actually do some major detecting, not just interview a crazy soccer coach."

"And he wasn't into it?"

"He was on his computer when I got there," Frank said. "I proposed the deal, and he seemed to think the idea was okay. But it wasn't what I expected, and that raised a red flag in my mind. The phone rang, and when he left the room to take the call, I carefully ran through some of the things on his desk. I found these."

Frank laid out three pieces of paper. They were computer printouts—one bio for each Hardy. "Look at the dates," Frank said.

"He ran these Wednesday," Joe concluded.

"But he said he didn't know who we were until he read the articles on Thursday," Frank said.

"We already know he lies," Joe pointed out.

"Yeah? Wait until you hear this," Frank said. "When

he got back to the room, he told me the call was from Isabelle, and she was sorry she'd brushed me off at the rally. He said she'd changed her mind about talking to me and was asking Jacques to set up a meet between Isabelle, you, and me. He said it was for eight o'clock tonight at Les Catacombes."

"Whoa," Joe said under his breath. He leaned back in his chair, picturing Isabelle being pushed away on the gurney and loaded into an ambulance. "No way she's calling him from the hospital."

"Exactly," Frank said. "He's setting us up."

"He's got to be in on all this somehow," Joe said. "Maybe he's one of Bergerac's people."

"Or he could be in Victoire, for all we know," Frank said, "and he's been setting us up from the very beginning—the rally, everything." Frank took a long gulp of soda.

"He could even be a lone wolf," Joe said.

"Well, I feel he's now the prime suspect for the sabotage at Le Stade," Frank said. "He also could have sent the e-mail from Dad." He felt a rush of adrenaline.

"So we roll tonight," Joe said, bringing his chair back down on all four legs, "no matter what."

"Into probably the worst trap we've ever been invited into," Frank said quietly.

Joe went to the counter at the front of the café and picked up a brochure with information about Les Catacombes. "It's like an underground tomb," he said. Frank ordered some *croque-monsieurs* while Joe filled him in.

"'In the late seventeen hundreds,'" Joe read, "'they quarried stone from under the streets and left these enormous vaults. The cemeteries were all over-crowded because of war and disease, so they moved millions of bodies from battlegrounds and other graveyards and hospital morgues to the catacombs.'"

"Millions?" Frank repeated.

"They added bodies for two hundred years, it says here," Joe read, "until there were eventually six million. Now it's a tourist attraction that closes at four o'clock in the afternoon most days."

"Except for people like us," Frank said. "Tonight we get our own exclusive look at Les Catacombes."

It was four o'clock when they finished eating. Frank placed his fifth call of the day to the symposium emergency number. The other times he'd talked to the same man who had called the night before. This time the call was answered by someone new, a woman with a kind, reassuring manner. She told Frank that all the conferees were working on locating Fenton Hardy, and no one was alarmed yet.

"He's working on a difficult case," she told Frank. "He might not check in as often as we'd like, but that doesn't mean he's in danger."

"Checking in often is never necessary," Frank said, after he'd repeated the conversation to Joe. "Just checking in once, though, would be a help."

"I'm with you," Joe said. "I'm thinking Jacques might be really dangerous. I don't like the idea of him messing with Dad. Let's get there early. I want every advantage we can get."

They returned to the apartment along the same path they believed Fenton had taken the day before and that Frank had retraced that morning. They repeated Frank's earlier efforts, showing shopkeepers and bus drivers a photo of their father and asking questions. No one had seen him the day before.

They got back to the apartment by about six o'clock. Frank checked for phone messages and e-mails, but there were none. Joe got out a map and they studied it carefully. Les Catacombes was located just a few steps from the Denfert-Rochereau Metro stop in the Montparnasse section of the city.

The Hardys memorized street and avenue names and other landmarks. They knew they had to be prepared to escape or to chase. And they had to know where they were going to be at all times.

"We can't take much with us," Frank said. "We need to be lean and mean; we can't have backpacks weighing us down."

"And no fancy spy gear for Jacques to steal," Joe added. "We'll just take one handheld."

"Do we know what we're getting ourselves into?" Frank asked. "He may have Victoire or Bergerac guys with him. Or he may be alone." Each teen tucked a lockpick into the bottom of his left sock. Joe slipped the handheld under his shirt, down below his jeans, and hid it behind his belt buckle. They were about the same size; if he got frisked, no one would feel the small device behind his buckle. Finally both Joe and Frank tucked penlights into their pockets.

"If he's by himself, he'll have to be armed," Frank reasoned, "because he knows we could take him. And he probably won't dare frisk us because if he gets in too close, he risks our jumping him."

By six forty-five they were ready. They took a couple of trains to the Denfert-Rochereau stop. As they walked from the train to the steps leading up to the street, Frank tried to picture the walls packed with bones. It was hard to imagine.

When they got to Les Catacombes, the area was deserted. The night was very dark. The full moon that had illuminated the lawn of Auguste Bergerac's chateau the previous evening was no help the next night. It was completely masked by thick clouds.

They walked around the area. "I studied that map so hard," Frank whispered, "that it all seems familiar."

They circled back to the entrance and were only slightly startled when Jacques materialized from the shadows with barely a sound.

"There you are," Joe said. "And alone."

"You don't seem surprised that it is me," Jacques observed. "So you had used your detective skills to put two and two together?"

"You made it easy," Frank said. "We've unearthed criminals far smarter than you."

"Now, boys, let's play nice, yes?" Jacques warned. He pulled his right arm up until his hand was lit by a streetlight. Clenched in his palm and glinting in the pale rays was a small revolver. He lowered his arm to his side again.

Frank felt an adrenaline rush. "This is your party, Jacques," he said. "What've you got in mind?"

Jacques motioned them forward with his head. The Hardys headed in the direction Jacques had indicated until he told them to stop. They were in front of a small secluded door to what looked like an ancient building. "This may look like an old door, but it's deceptive," Jacques said. "And its lock is regulated by a computer program. Open it."

Frank turned the knob, and the latch clicked.

"As you can see, I disabled it in preparation for our visit," Jacques said. "Go inside."

Frank pushed the door open, and he and Joe stepped into a large, dimly lit room. Jacques followed and closed the door. He ordered the Hardys to cross the room and walk down a narrow hall, until they finally came to a steep circular staircase leading sixty-five feet down to the catacombs.

He pushed them down the winding stairs. Then they turned into dimly lit narrow passages lined with bones; wall after wall of leg bones and arm bones stacked like bricks. In a few spots the Hardys saw designs created with skulls—hearts, flowers, and circles. The designs were made out of skulls.

On they walked, weaving through dozens of narrow tunnels, past thousands of bones. It seemed like a gruesome maze without a solution.

At last Jacques stopped the Hardys and turned them toward a darkened corridor with no bones in the walls. They moved forward until they came to a low door. Jacques shoved the Hardys through the opening. He turned on a flashlight that had been lying on the dirt floor. They were in a tiny room, sort of like an old-fashioned farm cellar.

"Where are we?" Frank demanded. He strained to see past the glow of the light beam.

"Hi, guys." A lump instantly filled Frank's throat when he heard his father's voice. He reached down and grabbed the flashlight, aiming it in the direction of a large shadowy mass in the corner.

The pale yellow light washed over a horrifying sight. Sticking up from a bank of dirt were Fenton Hardy's head and shoulders. He gave them a wry smile and nodded slowly.

Both Frank and Joe quickly turned back toward Jacques, but his grim expression and the gun in his hand told them it wouldn't do any good to argue with him. And it might do a lot worse to jump him.

"Have a seat, Frank, over by your father," Jacques ordered.

After Frank was settled, Jacques turned to Joe. "Now bury him," Jacques ordered.

Joe knew that for now he had no choice. He began shoveling dirt around his brother's legs.

"More," Jacques barked. "Higher—like I did with your dad."

Joe packed the dirt until Frank was buried up to his chest like his dad. Before his hands were covered, Frank slipped Joe his penlight. Joe tucked it in his jacket pocket without Jacques seeing.

When Frank was buried up to his chest, Jacques handcuffed both of Joe's hands to the iron ring handle inside the door. Then he picked up his flashlight. He left the room and slammed the door shut behind him. Joe could hear him on the other side, pushing something against the door. The Hardys were plunged into a rank, earthy blackness.

15 The Quarry in the Quarry

"Dad? Frank? Are you okay?" Joe twisted around a little. He could only turn partway from the door.

"Define 'okay,'" Fenton said in a weak voice.

"How long have you been here, Dad?" Frank asked. He tried to move his arms. Joe had done the best he could to make it a light packing of dirt, but Frank still could only wiggle his fingers and hands a little. He kept at it, but knew at this rate, it would take hours to free himself.

"I'm not sure," Fenton answered. "All day. It's time to get out."

"I'm working on it," Joe said. He twisted and contorted until he could get his jacket pocket near his fingers, which were trapped by the handcuffs. Inch by inch, he slowly pushed and pulled Frank's penlight from his jacket pocket and flicked it on. Then he dropped it to the floor. He pushed it around with his foot until it was propped up on a small mound of dirt.

The light helped a little. He saw his dad's face at the end of the light beam. Fenton looked pale and tired.

"Can you get to your pick?" Frank asked.

"I think so," Joe said, already pushing his sneaker off with the other foot. "I feel like something in a circus act."

He propped his leg up on the door near his handcuffed wrists. He positioned his fingers perfectly so he could strip off his sock and grab the lockpick before it fell to the dirt floor below.

It seemed to take hours to pick the handcuff lock because he had to twist his fingers into such difficult positions.

While Joe worked, Frank talked to Fenton. He could tell his dad was weak from going so long without food and water. He kept him awake by telling him about the Louvre secret passages, the houseboat, Isabelle Genet and Auguste Bergerac, and how their suspicions had grown about Jacques.

"How's it going, Joe?" Frank finally called from the shadowy corner of the little room. The dirt packed around him was beginning to drive him crazy. "This stuff is making me itch. It's probably the dozens of crawling things living in it."

"I've almost got it," Joe said. "Almost . . . there! I'm out." With a loud click, the cuffs fell away from his wrists. He rubbed his hands and fingers and headed right for the shovel.

Joe rushed over to unearth his father and brother. Fenton was weak and woozy. Once both Frank and the boys' father were free, Joe and Frank helped their dad move to the door of the little room. Jacques had firmly blocked the door, but the Hardys were determined. While Fenton held the penlight, Frank and Joe rammed into the door. It creaked open with a shower of dirt and rusty dust.

Jacques had pulled an iron bar from a brace shoring up the wall. He had jammed that against the door of the room to trap the Hardys.

Joe and Frank took a few moments to replace the bar on the ceiling, to ensure that the next visitors weren't showered with skulls. Then the three wound through the bone-lined maze of winding paths and finally arrived back at the circular staircase that led up to the street.

Once back in fresh air, Joe looked at his dad. "How are you doing?" he asked.

"I've been better," Fenton said. "But I think I've also been worse." He and Frank brushed from their clothes bits of dirt and pebbles. They left wet brown-black stains where they had clung.

"We need a cab," Frank said to his father. "You've got to get checked out by a doctor. Joe, you and

Dad stay here and rest. I'll go over to the boulevard and get a cab." From his map study earlier, Frank knew just which way to go to get to the busy street. A few cabs passed him by, but one finally stopped. He directed the driver back to where his father and Joe were resting.

"At last," Joe said.

"Yeah, well, a few didn't stop," Frank told them as they climbed in.

"I don't blame them," Fenton said, gesturing first to Frank and then himself. "We look like something that just crawled out of Les Catacombes."

"Les Catacombes . . . uumph," the cabby said with a shudder.

At the hospital Fenton quickly got attention. The doctors said he was badly dehydrated, chilled, and weak from hunger, but otherwise okay. He refused to stay for observation.

Frank insisted someone look at Joe's head wound. After the doctor cleaned and bandaged it, Joe was ready to get out of there too.

While his brother and father were being examined and mended, Frank paid a visit upstairs to Gabriel Sant'Anna. The coach was sitting up, able to talk, and happy to have a visitor.

"Do you remember the attack?" Frank asked.

"Yes, a little," Coach Sant'Anna answered. "I've told the police I saw the man only briefly before I lost consciousness."

Frank took out the folded-up paper he had taken from his first visit to that room. "Do you remember this note?" he asked. "And the message you wrote in blue pen on the locker room floor?"

"Yes—the police thought at first it was an *M*," Coach Sant'Anna said. "And they thought I was naming Montie Roberts." He chuckled. "I almost let them believe that too. But I couldn't, because it wasn't Montie. It could not have been Montie. He is a passionate man, but he is not violent."

"So were you writing a *W*?" Frank asked. "Or a *V*?"

"Yes, yes, a *V*," Coach Sant'Anna said, pointing to the letter on the paper. "Not just one *V*—two *V*s to make sure. You are the only one who figured that out." He waggled his finger at Frank. "You are very smart."

"And the *V* stands for . . . ," Frank prompted.

"Volunteer," said the coach. "It was one of the volunteers who jumped me. I had seen him on the field."

Frank described Jacques, and the coach nodded. "That could definitely be the man," he agreed. "Perhaps I will recognize him if I see him."

"We'll try to arrange that," Frank said with a smile. He thanked the coach and rejoined Joe and Fenton in the emergency room.

Frank told the others what he'd learned from Coach Sant'Anna. Then Fenton called his security colleagues and told them everything the Hardys knew about Jacques.

"They're putting out a bulletin on him," Fenton told his sons when he hung up the phone. "I expect he'll be picked up before morning."

"I say we celebrate," Joe said. "We're all okay, we might be about to crack a case, and we're in Paris. How about some dinner?"

"I'm meeting with some of my colleagues," Fenton said, shaking his head. "After all, I'm a prime witness, and I want to be in on the capture."

"We should go too," Frank said. "I've got a few bones to pick with him myself." Fenton and Joe groaned when they heard the play on words.

"Nice try," their father said. "But this guy's more than dangerous, I think. He's a little nuts. We've got a lot of people on this. I'm sure we'll get him . . . and we'll do it without putting you two in danger. I'll keep you posted."

After Fenton left, Joe talked to one of the nurses. He told her their friend Isabelle Genet was in a hospital in Montmartre, and asked if the nurse could call over there and find out how she was doing. The nurse placed the call. She found out that Isabelle was in serious condition, but would recover.

Frank needed to change out of his filthy, stained clothes, so they headed back to the apartment for a cleanup. While Frank changed, Fenton called. He told Joe that they still hadn't picked up Jacques, but hoped to soon.

"I say we set our own trap," Joe said. After checking

the guidebooks and maps, they agreed on a plan. Joe set up the high-tech voice alterer. Frank called Jacques's cell phone. Someone accepted the call, but no one spoke. Figuring that Jacques was on the other end but didn't want to give himself away, Frank spoke without waiting for a response. He knew the voice alterer would disguise the sound so that Jacques would not know who was calling.

"Monsieur Ravel," Frank said, "I am calling as a representative from Victoire. You do not need to know my name. We know everything about you. We know you are the Le Stade saboteur and that the authorities also know this. We also know that you are close to being captured by undercover agents."

Joe gave his brother the thumbs up sign, and Frank continued. "If you join our cause and work underground as a computer expert for Victoire, we will protect you and hide you from the authorities. We have many safe havens for you to use. You need to make your decision quickly. I am telling you that you have little time left as a free man unless you join with us. Meet with me; you will not be sorry."

"Le parc des Buttes-Chaumont in one half hour," Jacques said in a low voice. "The bridge on the west side." Then he hung up.

The Hardys scrambled for their guidebooks. "Here it is," Joe said. "It's in an old quarry." They studied the book for a few minutes. "Come on," Joe urged. "We have to beat him there if we can."

They packed up and left the apartment. The Metro stopped right next to the park. Located in a gigantic excavated gypsum quarry, Parc Buttes-Chaumont was one of the largest parks in Paris. The surrounding neighborhood was called *Carrières d'Amérique*—American Quarries—because so much of the stone from there went to the United States.

Now Buttes-Chaumont was a canyon with patches of woods, steep cliffs, waterfalls, and caves. Two suspension footbridges swung high above a lake, connecting the outer edge of the park with a tall island butte in the middle of the water. Once the Hardys arrived, they hid in the lush trees near the west bridge.

The moon, having emerged from the clouds, was still nearly full and a bright yellow-white color. It was dark in the surrounding canyon, but the suspension footbridge and the small lake far below could be seen in the light.

The Hardys waited for fifteen minutes, then a half hour, then ten minutes more. "He should have been here by now," Frank whispered. "He's late."

"He's here," Joe said. "He's here somewhere. I just know it. He's probably hidden in the trees like us, waiting until he sees the Victoire guy."

There weren't many people in the park at this late hour. A few couples strolled in the moonlight at the top of the cliffs, and customers drank tea at a café that clung to the wall of the canyon. In the distance, a man rowed a canoe slowly through the moonlight.

"There he is," Frank said, nodding to the opposite end of the bridge. Jacques stood on the clifflike butte in the middle of the lake.

"We should have both ends of the bridge covered," Joe said. "That way we can trap him in the middle."

"Remember, he might be armed," Frank said.

"So far he hasn't killed anybody," Joe reasoned. "And the bridge is out in the open in the moonlight, where everyone can see him. He's probably not going to try anything extreme out there."

"Okay, get going," Frank said. "I'll give you a few minutes, then start talking to him. But be careful. Dad thinks he might be insane—and I'd agree."

Joe first backed out of the trees, then started around to the other side of the bridge. Frank couldn't see his brother, but he watched around the rim of the canyon, visualizing where Joe would probably be.

He also kept his eye on Jacques across the way. Jacques was like a nervous rabbit, standing on the bridge for a few minutes, then ducking back into the foliage, then moving back out on the bridge, then running back into the woods.

When he figured that Joe was more than halfway to the other end of the bridge, Frank was ready. He waited until Jacques made another appearance, then Frank stepped out of his hiding place onto his end of the bridge.

Jacques looked stunned. He then laughed out loud and began walking slowly across the bridge.

Frank scanned the area. Customers were still coming and going at the café, and a few people were strolling along the cliffs or sitting on benches near the edge of the lake. The canoer was still gliding along. Everyone had looked up when Jacques laughed.

"Too many witnesses," Frank told himself. "He's not going to try anything here."

Frank stepped out onto the bridge and walked slowly toward Jacques. *Hurry up, Joe,* he thought.

Joe raced through the woods and over to the other side of the bridge. As he snuck up behind Jacques, he saw Frank across the lake.

Joe crouched down behind a flowering shrub and watched for a moment. Frank and Jacques walked slowly toward each other. Jacques patted his pocket a couple of times. *He's trying to indicate that he's got a weapon,* Joe said.

Still crouching, Joe crept toward the bridge. *As soon as I step on the bridge, he's going to feel it,* Joe thought. *Okay, here goes.* He stood up and stepped onto the bridge. It swayed slightly. A few yards ahead, Jacques wheeled around. In the pale light, his eyes looked black, and his face an angry purple.

Joe didn't give him a chance to think. First he delivered a perfect karate kick on Jacques's bicep, driving his opponent's hand away from the loaded pocket. Then he lunged for Jacques, tackling him hard and jamming him to the floor of the swinging bridge.

Jacques twisted his legs out of Joe's grip and scrambled back to his feet. Frank moved quickly toward them from the other side, his footsteps swaying the bridge. Jacques reached again for his pocket, but Joe landed a strong uppercut to Jacques's chin.

With a furious *aaaangh* sound, Jacques leaped straight at Joe, pushing him toward the edge of the bridge. His hands reached forward, fingers curling. Joe felt the thin handrail in his back as Jacques's fingers closed around his neck. He brought both arms up to break the hold. With a shock, he felt his balance shift as he and his attacker leaned farther over the edge of the bridge.

16 Kickoff!

Jacques's fingers tightened around Joe's neck as the two of them leaned farther off the bridge and out over the lake. Several people from below cried out in horror.

Joe butted his head forward to regain his balance. Then he brought both arms up hard, breaking Jacques's grip. With a panicked expression, Jacques looked around, then turned toward the end of the bridge from which he started.

But Joe didn't like that idea. He crouched, spun, and planted another pinpoint karate kick to Jacques's legs, whipping them out from under him. With a shaking thud, Jacques fell on his face. This was Frank's cue to meet his brother.

"You okay, Joe?" Frank asked as he handcuffed Jacques to the handrail.

Joe nodded and rubbed his neck. He called his father with the handheld, and Frank carefully took the gun form Jacques's pocket.

While they waited for Fenton, Frank pumped Jacques for answers. Joe turned on his microphone/recorder for good measure. At first Jacques was belligerent and refused to talk. But when Frank pretended to admire Jacques's hacking prowess, he started to open up.

"Yes, I broke into the computer program of the Macri Magnifico fireworks company," Jacques bragged. "I changed the trajectory of more than one firework. And the changes were brilliant. My only regret is that the results were wasted on the rehearsal. How much more fun it would have been with a packed house of a hundred thousand."

"You almost got your wish," Frank said. "They were set to do the fireworks the next night."

"Yes, and the changes in the computer programs are still there," Jacques said, smiling. He had dropped the surly attitude. "But I was so sure they'd cancel the fireworks for the opening ceremonies that I hacked into the night lighting system."

"Sort of overkill, don't you think?" Joe observed. "When the lights exploded, the fireworks display was postponed again."

"Yes, but it also postponed the tournament for a while," Jacques said, "which was an unexpected benefit."

"But it's back on now," Joe said. "We report at nine o'clock tomorrow morning."

"If you dare," Jacques responded. He smiled at Joe.

"And what does that mean?" Joe asked.

"I think maybe Jacques is hinting at other surprises he's plotted," Frank said.

"There's one thing I can't figure out," Joe said. "What's in this for you, Jacques? What are you getting out of it?"

Jacques stopped grinning and pulled up straight. "I'm the best there is," he said. "The reigning king of computing in Paris—maybe in all of France! It was time for advancement. Time to widen my reputation. I know I'm one of the premier hackers in the world. It's time the rest of the international community knew it."

"And what better venue could you have to show off your skills," Joe pointed out, "than an international event in a world capital?"

"What about Coach Sant'Anna?" asked Frank. "You're the one who attacked him, aren't you?"

"Yes, I am," Jacques answered. "First I needed a diversion for the police and stadium guards. Something to keep them occupied while I sabotaged the fireworks. Plus it was fun setting up old Magnificent

Montie," he added. "It wasn't at all difficult to make everyone think he was the culprit."

"Did you knock out Coach Sant'Anna and then lure Coach Roberts to the locker room?" Joe asked, leading the witness.

"Yes," Jacques nodded. "And I even hoped to make a little cash on the deal. I intended to blackmail Montie by pretending to discover him with Sant'Anna's body. I figured he'd pay me to keep quiet. He's been in so much trouble, it won't take many more incidents to ensure that he's banned from the sport for life. I wasn't counting on you arriving to disrupt my little side deal," he said to Frank.

"So you're the one who popped in and then slammed out right after I got there," Frank said.

"That's right," Jacques said.

"What about this?" Frank took the golden walnut charm from his pocked and showed it to Jacques.

"*You* found it," Jacques said. "Oh . . . that's what you were talking about yesterday when you gave me that little assignment. Having me interview Montie and ask him if he's misplaced anything— that was a little test. I wondered why the police hadn't mentioned it; it's because you found it."

"Did you drop it at the Macri Magnifico compound?" Joe asked.

"Yes," Jacques said. "I had to keep the heat on Montie, so I stole it from him and dropped it near the fireworks compound."

"How did you figure this all out?" Jacques asked. "How did you know it was me?"

Frank told him about catching all the lies. "The clincher was you telling us that Isabelle had called to set up a meeting tonight," he concluded.

"I went to Isabelle Genet's house this afternoon," Joe said. "I found her in the trunk."

"I guess this means that all my traps have been sprung," Jacques said with a grin. "Looks like everyone's free again."

"Everyone but you," Joe said.

Jacques looked out over the lake. "Isabelle was very useful as a diversion for a while," he added, "she and that motley crew Victoire. . . . But she'd begun to get in the way. She has some plans up her sleeve, you know. I'm not the only guilty party."

"We're on it, thanks," Frank said.

"She and her whole gang of ruffians had thoroughly outlived their usefulness to me," Jacques said. "It was time to send them all a little warning. Le Stade is my turf; they need to find their own playground."

"What about Dad?" Joe asked. "What's with that?"

"I grant you, kidnapping your father seems to have been a mistake," Jacques said. "I knew about the security symposium, of course. I accessed some of the records, although I haven't been able to get into the really juicy ones yet. I saw his name on the invitation list, so I knew he was in town."

Jacques shrugged his shoulders. "It was just a matter of time," he said. "I had the feeling you two were getting close to figuring out my real identity and purpose. I assumed your father would know next, and then the entire symposium. Grabbing him was a spur-of-the-moment decision. I knew he would be great bait for you two, and I thought I could tuck you all away in Les Catacombes—for a *long* time."

"Someone talking about me?" Fenton asked. He stepped onto the bridge and was followed by several men and women.

"Looks like my sons have done the hard work here," Fenton said with a proud smile. "You two don't mind if we take over the cleanup?"

"Be our guest," Frank said, grinning. "We'll see you later."

Jacques was placed under arrest and taken away by Fenton and the others.

Frank and Joe grabbed some savory crepes on the way home. Once they got to the apartment, they took their food to the kitchen. They were still eating when Fenton arrived.

"You did a great job, guys," he said, sitting down to join them. "Not only is Jacques under wraps, but we've rounded up some of the Victoire people too."

"Starting with Gaston, I hope," Joe said, remembering the dogs he aggravated at Bergerac's estate.

"Yes," Fenton nodded. "And Isabelle Genet is

improving, so we'll be able to begin questioning her tomorrow. Some heavyweights in international security are also going to talk to Bergerac."

"Jacques hinted that he still has bugs in some of the computer programs at Le Stade," Frank said.

"He was bragging about that to us, too," Fenton said. "Until our own techie can find and undo all his dirty work, the tournament has been moved to le parc des Princes stadium across town. You report there with the other volunteers at nine tomorrow morning," he said, checking his watch, "which gives you not nearly enough time to sleep! Welcome to the world of detectives, right? Good night." With their father's parting works, Frank and Joe decided to call it a night.

Sunday morning was a beautiful day for soccer. When the Hardys arrived at the tournament's new venue, they were greeted with a rousing cheer. Everyone had read about their daring capture of Jacques Ravel in the morning tabloid. And this time they were all grateful—even Montie Roberts.

"Great job, guys," he boomed, clapping both Hardys on the back with his big hands. Frank reached into his pocket and pulled out the golden walnut charm. He handed it to Montie, who responded with a punch of gratitude on Frank's shoulder.

Even Coach Sant'Anna was back on the field. He

was in a wheelchair, but he was ready to get back to work. "We are all in your debt," he told the Hardys.

"Hey, we just followed the rules of soccer," Frank pointed out. "Fight for the advantage, call the fouls when you see them, defend yourself against a breakaway—"

"And keep the ball in play until you score," Joe added with a grin.